Hiding From Danger

Georgette "Gigi" Sidney is a woman on the run. Her ex-boyfriend's love was controlling, obsessive, and deadly. Now she's hiding out in Tremont, Montana spending her days as a waitress and her nights in West Anderson's bed. She ought to be moving on to the next town but her feelings for the handsome detective have complicated her plans.

Everything in life has come easily for West Anderson. Until now. Despite the passionate nights he and Gigi have shared she's constantly talking about leaving town. He knows she has some sort of a secret but so far she hasn't trusted him enough to reveal it.

When Gigi's past interferes with the present she has to finally tell West the truth…about everything. She needs twenty-four hour protection and he's just the man for the job.

If West has his way there will be no more running, no more excuses, and no more lies. He's determined to put the past to rest so that he can be her future. All he has to do is catch a madman and keep her alive while doing it.

Hiding From Danger

Danger Incorporated

Book Two

BY

OLIVIA JAYMES

www.OliviaJaymes.com

HIDING FROM DANGER

Print Edition

Copyright © 2015 by Olivia Jaymes

Chapter One

GEORGETTE "GIGI" SIDNEY ran her fingers down Westin Anderson's spine, his skin smooth and warm to the touch. Her limbs still languid and her mind fuzzy after the lovemaking they'd shared mere moments before, he'd tucked her into the curve of his body with her head pillowed on his bicep and his leg thrown over her possessively.

No. Not making love. Sex. It was just sex.

Awesome sex, though. Off the charts amazing. West knew all the little spots that were designed to make a woman writhe, moan, and scream with pleasure. An unselfish lover, he'd taught her what sex was really supposed to be like. Before him she simply hadn't seen what all the fuss was about.

West's fingers wound around strands of her long hair before gently tugging her head back until she was looking into those moss green eyes fringed in enviable thick dark lashes. When he smiled a dimple pierced his right cheek, making him look not only handsome but charming as well. By any standards he was gorgeous, just like all the Anderson boys.

But at this particular moment he wasn't smiling at all, instead looking down at her as if trying to study her features and answer some deep, burning question inside of him.

Questions she couldn't even begin to answer. There were some things West Anderson could never know.

"Are you thirsty?" he finally asked, and she inwardly sighed in relief that he wasn't going to push her tonight. The last time she'd come over to his house they'd ended up arguing. She didn't want to ruin the pleasant afterglow of what they'd shared. "I can get us a couple of beers."

Every cell of her body wanted to stay here with him. Share a beer and watch a movie. Laugh about the interesting characters that frequented the diner where she worked as a waitress. Hear about West's day running his campaign for mayor of Tremont. Simple pleasures and a simple life.

But nothing about her life was uncomplicated. She'd left that far behind long ago.

"I should be going." Her legs still like jelly and her heart beating fast, Gigi shook her head and attempted to extricate herself from the tangle of arms and legs they'd become after their spectacular simultaneous orgasms. She'd thought they'd only existed in books. "I have the early shift at the diner."

"You always have the early shift. And the late shift too."

West didn't sound pissed off about it. More curious than anything. But then he was the son of one of the richest men in Montana, if not the entire western United States. Desperately needing money probably wasn't something he'd ever experienced.

"You know what they say…idle hands and all that," she replied lightly. "Besides, the breakfast shift has the best tips. A girl needs pretty things, you know."

Gigi rarely allowed herself indulgences with her hard-earned money, so West's disbelieving expression wasn't all that much of a surprise.

"I'd be happy to buy you something pretty if I thought you wouldn't toss it back in my face and then knee me in the balls."

Giggling at his laconic tone Gigi sat up, pulling the sheet over her bare breasts. She'd been engaging in sex with West for almost three months now but she still wasn't used to his hungry gaze on her naked body. He looked at her like he wanted to eat her up.

Which in and of itself wasn't a bad thing.

It was the emotions that went along with it that made her weak, something she couldn't allow to happen.

"Would I be the first? Is there a long line of scorned women out there wishing they could hit you where it counts?"

"Hell, no." West wore a scowl on his handsome face. "What kind of guy do you think I am? There haven't been that many women, babe."

"Are you sure?" Gigi arched an eyebrow and tried to suppress a smile. "Practically the first thing I was told when I took that waitress job was to watch out for West Anderson's playboy ways. They told me that even before they showed me the menu or how to work the coffee pot."

And yet she'd fallen into bed with him without much work on his part.

West swung his legs to the floor and stood there bare ass naked. It was easy to see what all the women in Tremont – plus a good part of the entire state of Montana – saw in him. Sex on legs, every inch of him was chiseled from the finest marble. Just his presence was enough to make her tingle.

And that's why she had to leave. Not just his bed but Tremont all together. She'd already spent far more time here than she'd planned. He'd wriggled under her skin and made her do things she wouldn't normally do.

"I've dated my share of women but not as many as people think." Hands on his lean hips, West's eyes were narrowed with frustration. "Not that any of them matter right now. They're in the past."

Implying that she was the present? And maybe the future?

Uh uh. No way. The walls felt like they were closing in on her, making it hard to even take a breath. He'd been doing this lately…talking about them as if they were a couple. Like they were dating or something.

"You're right, it doesn't matter." Gigi shrugged nonchalantly and reached down to the floor to scoop up her discarded clothing. She kept her voice casual despite the acid churning in her stomach. "We're just friends with benefits. Fuck buddies. I don't have any strings on you, West. You can have all the women your heart desires as many times as you please."

✦   ✦   ✦

THAT WAS THE problem.

West didn't want any other women. He wanted Gigi. And at times he was pretty sure she wanted him too. Other times he didn't think she cared for him at all unless it was about sex.

The entire situation was ironic enough to make even him laugh if he wasn't so damn frustrated twenty-four hours a day.

West hadn't had to lift a finger to get a woman to chase him since he was fourteen years old and his braces came off. The fact was most things had come easily to him. Women. Sports. The military. And now being a cop.

But if he wanted Gigi he was going to have to work to get her. She was skittish and wary. Someone, somewhere had done a number on his girl. She didn't trust easily or much at all, really. Even now after three months of dating she wouldn't spend the night in his bed. With any woman before her he wouldn't have minded but he missed her warm little body curled up close to his.

"I'd say we're looking at fuck buddies in the rear view mirror, babe."

West grabbed his boxers and pulled them on, a cool breeze drying the sweat on his skin. He'd left the windows cracked to let in some fresh air and the temperature had dropped several degrees since the sun went down.

Gigi's shoulders stiffened and she pulled the sheet up almost to her neck. Too late. He'd seen every delicious inch of Ms. Sidney and committed every curve to memory. "We made a deal. No relationship. No emotions. Just sex."

"How's that working out for you?" West padded across the room and shut the window, twisting the lock tight out of habit. He was a cop, after all. "We both know that deal got blown out of the water after the first month we were together. Does it scare you to give a shit?"

West tried to keep the impatience out of his tone. Whatever Gigi was terrified of wasn't her fault. Some guy had probably been a complete dick and broken her heart fucking some other girl leaving West to pick up the pieces and try to prove to her that all guys weren't complete pigs.

Except that West had been a total hound dog until he met her. But it hadn't taken him long at all to see that Gigi wouldn't put up with any of his shit for one minute. She would have turned her back and been long gone. Suddenly acting like a jerk and having women pant over him didn't seem as cool as it once had.

She tugged on her clothes, her movements jerky and her lips pressed tight together. *Awesome.* She was pissed at him.

"This wasn't part of the plan. None of this. I told you I can't do any more. You're asking too much, West. Can't this be enough for you?"

She'd told him in the beginning but not as to why she wanted to keep it low key and casual. That's what they'd argued about the other night and he didn't want a repeat performance.

"Is it enough for you?" he countered. "You care, Gigi. Or you would if you let yourself. You're not just another piece of ass to me."

Apparently this wasn't good news.

Sighing, she shoved a foot into a beaten up sneaker that should have been replaced a long time ago. He would have done it himself but she was so damn independent.

"I can't do this and frankly I'm too tired to argue." She finished tying her shoe and stood next to the bed they'd made love in. Where she'd given herself to him but always with reservation. She held a part of herself back and it only served to make him want it more. "I won't be in Tremont forever, West. I told you that in the beginning."

His chest tightened with fear. He couldn't say she hadn't

warned him because she had. But he wasn't an idiot. He knew when a female had feelings for him. He could see it in her eyes when they shared a pizza and laughed. He could feel it in the way she touched him, almost reverently as if he was the first man she'd ever been with. He could hear it in her voice when she said his name.

Gigi was scared and frankly so was he. Scared that she wouldn't stick around long enough for him to prove she didn't have anything to be afraid of. He wasn't planning on hurting her. He only wanted a chance to get closer. Find out more and see if maybe this thing between them had a future.

And he'd sure as shit never felt that way before.

"Why would you want to leave Tremont? I thought you liked your job and the town."

He could tell she was about to lie to him when she swallowed hard, her cheeks turning pink. "I told you in the beginning that I like to move around. I don't stay in one place long and I've been here almost four months. I'm not leaving tomorrow but eventually I'll go. There's no future with me. I don't think I'm capable of feeling deeply for anyone if you must know."

"Bullshit. Do you actually believe what comes out of your mouth? I don't. Don't take up poker, babe, because your expression says one thing and your words say something else. Right now, I don't think you're all that thrilled about leaving Tremont. I think you'd rather slip back between those sheets with me and see what we can get up to before falling fast asleep. If you spend the night I'll make you bacon and eggs for breakfast."

Even as the words had tumbled out he knew he was fucking

7

this all up. He was pushing and it was only making her more frightened, ready to bolt. He needed to back off and give her space.

"I don't want to argue with you. I'm going home."

Gigi swung her purse over her shoulder and headed out of the bedroom practically racing for the front door. With his much longer legs, he was able to easily catch up to her, and he placed his hand on the door knob over hers, the heat from her skin searing his own flesh.

"I'm sorry, okay?" His finger tightened around hers and he looked down into her unusual amber colored eyes, her long blonde hair disheveled around her shoulders, making her look infinitely kissable. "Listen, I don't want to fight either. Tonight was too good to let it end this way."

West dropped his voice to a whisper, his fingers trailing up the satin skin of her arm. He felt her shiver and her lips parted in a half sigh of pleasure. She might not want West but she definitely wanted what he could do to her.

"I don't either. But I do need to go. Really."

There was a plea in her voice that tugged at his heart. "I'll drive you home."

Gigi shook her head, that determined gleam back in her eyes. "I have my own car. I'll be fine."

"That's not the point but I'll give in gracefully. This time."

He didn't try and stop her from opening the door. A cool gust of wind wafted around them bringing her clean scent to his nostrils, like fresh rain with a hint of soap. It turned him on far more than any expensive perfume or lotion.

"Good night, West."

She was already down his porch steps and opening her car door.

"Good night, Gigi. I'll see you tomorrow."

He meant it as a promise. He'd be sitting in his usual booth at seven-thirty in the morning. If he couldn't wake up with her in his bed this was the next best thing.

She didn't reply again, climbing into her old vehicle and backing out of his driveway before heading down the quiet street. Most of the neighbors had turned in for the night long ago.

He stood in the doorway and watched her red taillights until they disappeared into the distance. What had started out as something casual and light had turned into something far different. Surprisingly West wasn't running scared despite many years of keeping women from getting too serious. He was almost forty and it was honestly past time to find a good woman.

Gigi Sidney was one of the best.

Obviously she didn't feel the same. But then West had never been a quitter. If she wasn't sure about him then he'd simply have to show her how good they could be together.

He only needed time.

Chapter Two

GIGI STOPPED AT the red light, blinking back a few unwelcome tears. After all this time she ought to be used to it. Making friends and then leaving them behind. Except that West was much more than just a friend. She'd let him in farther than anyone and that was where she'd gone wrong. If she'd kept him at arm's length like all the others that had drifted in and out of her life she wouldn't be in this mess.

When the light turned green, she pulled away from the intersection still lost in her self-pitying thoughts. If she had any sense at all she'd leave Tremont soon. Nothing good could come from hanging around longer. Tonight she'd log on to her old laptop and look for the next place. There would always be another town, each one different but mostly the same. With any luck she'd blend into the background of daily life until it was time to move on again.

This was her life and crying and sniffling didn't make a damn bit of difference.

Pulling her back to the present, the car behind her threw their high beams into her mirror creating a blinding glare that made her momentarily swerve. Stone cold fear stopped her heart for a split second before starting again, this time beating so fast she thought it might fly out of her chest. She squinted her eyes but couldn't make out even the shape of the driver in the vehicle.

Stay calm. It's probably just some kids.

The unknown auto had materialized out of the darkness and was now right behind her revving its engine impatiently. Her fingers tightening on the steering wheel, she glanced again into the rearview. This time she was able to make out the metallic grill of a large pickup truck right on her tail. The driver pulled close…then slowed down…lengthening the distance between their bumpers. She breathed a sigh of relief but it was short-lived. The unseen driver gunned the engine and was right on the ass of her car again.

Just stay cool. Don't panic.

Feeling faint, she took a deep steadying breath and pressed on the accelerator. The old car whined in protest but the needle on the speedometer slowly climbed until she was fifteen over the speed limit. The truck didn't budge from her bumper and the reflection from the headlights still made it hard to see.

Okay, that didn't work. Now what?

With more than a small amount of joy, Gigi glimpsed the twenty-four hour convenience store on the next block. Lit up and friendly, it was just the oasis she'd been praying for. She quickly turned into the parking lot, her sweaty palms slick on the steering wheel, and watched as the pickup truck barreled past the store and into the night.

Still shaking with fright, she pressed her face into her hands and finally let the tears that had been threatening since she'd left West slide down her cheeks. She hated living like this. Scared every single second of every single day. Always on the run. She didn't know what she'd done in a past life to get shit on this way in this one but here she was.

Alone.

Alive.

For now.

When the chips were down the only person she could count on was herself. She'd known that for a long time although every now and then she had to remind herself. Tonight was one of those times. She longed to have someone she could lean on and trust but that only led to disappointment later. It was better to know the truth up front.

This episode with the truck had been a stark reminder of reality. Life was hard.

It was time to plan her next move. It was time to say goodbye to West and Tremont.

✦   ✦   ✦

WEST FLIPPED ON the television and slid between the covers of his bed, Gigi's scent still clinging to the sheets and pillow case. She was stubborn and he was damn frustrated about the entire situation. Was he so unattractive that she couldn't even consider sticking around? Was he only good enough to make her come but not to be cared about?

It stunk.

It also gave him an entirely new appreciation for the beautiful ladies who had professed to him their desire for a "real" relationship. He wished he'd handled it better and more sensitively than he had.

West's phone on the night stand lit up and he sighed in resignation. He might be on leave from the Tremont Police force but as the Head of Detectives he still received calls from his men regarding cases in progress.

He swiped his thumb across the screen. "Anderson."

"Good. You're awake."

Travis Anderson was West's oldest brother and the man that ran the family business holdings. He was also helping out on West's campaign to unseat the current asshole of a mayor which was probably the subject of this call.

"What would you have done if I'd been asleep?"

"I assume you wouldn't have answered the phone so I would have left a message. Am I wrong?"

"I'm a cop. I don't turn off my phone."

West wasn't pissed that Travis had called actually. He needed to talk to someone even if it was only about the campaign or the weather. He'd never liked to be alone all that much. It probably came from being raised in a house full of siblings and cousins. Living alone didn't seem quite natural.

"Noted. Listen, I got a tip there's going to be a story in tomorrow's paper about a case you worked a few years ago. The Loenel murder. I want you to be ready to counter their claims that you railroaded an innocent man to prison."

West couldn't hold back a loud snort of derision. Mayor Leon Cavendish must be getting mighty fucking desperate. "Innocent? Michael Cleaver had a list of priors a mile long plus a motive. And he was caught with the bloody knife in his hand, leaning over the body plunging it in Leonel's chest over and over again. Other than the fact that Cleaver kept saying he was framed, it was an open and shut case."

"Well I guess he's sticking to that story and giving out jail-house interviews now. I just thought you should know. Put together a quote and we'll get it to the press first thing in the morning."

The "press" in Tremont consisted of a guy named Earl and when he was sick or on vacation a woman named Sarah who also wrote a column in the paper about gardening. Travis had obviously spent too much time in New York City lately.

"I'll take care of it."

"Good. Now tell me why you're awake this late. Woman troubles, bro?"

West didn't appreciate the amused tone in Travis's voice but then West had been pretty tough on Travis and Jason in the past. The three brothers were always busting each other's balls about one thing or another.

"Everything is fine. Gigi just left. She has an early shift at the diner."

"Your words say one thing but the sound of your voice says something all together different. Did you two have a fight?"

"No. Yes. Maybe. Shit, I don't know. She's not like any other woman I've dated in the past."

"Is that a good or a bad thing?" Already irritated by Gigi's exit, West could hear his brother laughing. "I like Gigi. She's a tough one. Doesn't take any crap from anybody. Yesterday she verbally slapped down some cowboy who tried to cop a feel while she was taking his order."

This was the first West was hearing about it. He'd have to ask her who it was and have a serious talk with the offending male.

"This whole relationship started out to be more like friends with benefits than a love affair but somewhere along the line I've really come to care for her."

"I take it she's not on board with the change in direction? Is that why she left your house in the middle of the night?"

"I guess so," West admitted. "I've never had a female keep me at arm's length like this."

"So court her. Pitch some woo, bro. Be charming and romantic. Do all her favorite things and bowl her over."

"The thing is I don't know all that much about Gigi. She's so…"

"Secretive?" Travis prompted. "You told me once she didn't like to talk about her past but after all this time you still haven't found out anything?"

What West knew about Gigi was actually quite pathetic. Every time he tried to get to know her better she somehow managed to change the subject until he forgot what he was trying to do.

"Not really. When I've tried to find out her favorite movie or book she turns the question around on me and the next thing I know we're having sex."

Now that he was thinking about it, Gigi had managed to stop any personal conversations in their tracks all by using his libido against him.

"Some men wouldn't think that's a problem."

"It wasn't at first. But now…"

Travis took so long to respond West thought that the call had dropped. "You could have Jason do a little research into

Miss Sidney. Nothing in depth but just some general background."

"No way. I wouldn't do that to her. If she has something she doesn't want me to know I won't intrude on her privacy."

No matter how tempting it might be. He was a jerk but not an asshole.

"Then you're going to have to work even harder and stop having sex long enough to talk to her. You're a cop so you should know how to be sneaky and find things out without seeming to be interrogating her."

"I tend not to treat my girlfriends like suspects. It makes things go more smoothly." West didn't bother to keep the sarcasm out of his voice. "For a wise older brother, you aren't being much help."

"What the hell do I know about relationships? You want sex advice? I can help there. But love and the more tender emotions? Sorry. You might want to talk to Jason. He might be able to offer some suggestions."

It was bad enough talking to Travis about this without adding Jason into the humiliating mix.

"I can handle this on my own. No family intervention needed. Just stick to worrying about my campaign and leave my love life to me."

"Got it. No telling mom and dad." West almost clutched his chest at the thought of discussing his love life with his parents. They were wonderful people but he sure as hell didn't want to talk about sex and...feelings...with the people who still remembered when he wore diapers. "Listen, I'm beat. I'll call you tomorrow about the press release. Get some rest, okay? We have that visit to the shops on Main Street tomorrow. You're the champion of small business, remember?"

It wasn't likely he would forget. The entire reason he was running for mayor was to get rid of the corrupt town government currently in power. They were crushing the little guy in favor of big money and corporate interests.

"I'm tired too. Why don't you meet me for breakfast at the diner? Seven-thirty?"

"Sounds good. See you then."

Travis rung off and West placed the phone back on the nightstand before flipping off the bedside lamp. He left the television on and zoomed up the volume. He knew himself well enough to know he wouldn't be falling asleep for awhile. His mind was too active, working on the puzzle that was Gigi.

With everything going on in his life he might do better to let the relationship die a natural death. She was clearly pulling away and honestly he should probably allow her to do it. Stop fighting the inevitable and find someone who didn't look for reasons to push him away.

Before he did something stupid like fall in love.

Chapter Three

THE SUN WAS barely up the next morning and the parking lot of Gigi's apartment complex was deserted, the hour too early for most. After the incident last night, she needed to be sure she was ready to leave at a moment's notice even if she didn't have time to make it back to her place. She'd grown lazy and inattentive since she'd come here to Tremont but she'd be sharper now. Fear was a powerful motivator.

Unlocking the door, Gigi reached under the driver's seat of her piece of shit car. She ran her fingers along a rip in the fabric until she felt the corner of an envelope she'd tucked up into the upholstery and springs.

Got it.

She quickly retrieved the envelope before climbing into the car and locking the door behind her. It was an ingrained habit now. Even in a small town like this, she didn't feel safe without a barred door between herself and the world.

A prison of her own making. Ironic.

Holding the envelope below window-level, she quickly counted the bills tucked inside. Fifteen hundred dollars, and hopefully another hundred at the end of this week. It had taken months of scrimping and saving to get her stash that high. Her clothes were falling apart along with her vehicle but she'd learned to do without. At one time she'd hoped to save enough to hire a private detective to help her but she'd realized they were way out of her price range. She had to do the best she could alone.

Balancing the stack of bills on her thigh, she checked the additional items. Just to make herself feel better. It was compulsive behavior but she lived in terror of losing any of her important papers. That's why she kept them hidden and locked in her car instead of in her apartment or even shoved into her purse.

Driver's license. Birth certificate. Passport. Social Security card.

She breathed easier simply holding them in her hands. Tucking everything back in, she reached underneath the seat and slid it back into its spot. If she needed to leave she was ready.

She dug her car keys out of her purse and fired up the engine. She was due on shift in fifteen minutes, and if she knew West Anderson, he would show up for breakfast and sit in her section. It was hard to imagine a day when she wouldn't see him anymore. He'd become such an integral part of her life these last three months.

Gigi would miss him. And admitting that hurt more than anything.

✦   ✦   ✦

GIGI RUBBED HER throbbing temple and stretched in the uncomfortable wooden chair. She'd been sitting in the Tremont Library using its free Wi-Fi for the last hour and a half. Her head hurt, her butt was numb, and her shoulders ached. This after an eight hour shift on her feet at the diner.

She was exhausted.

West had invited her over to his place but she'd refused. Not because she didn't want to go. She did. But she had work to do, and he couldn't be a part of that. A good night's sleep wouldn't hurt either.

She clicked on another link from her search results. She was pages upon pages deep and she doubted most people ever had the patience to go this far. Scanning the page, she sighed and clicked the back button. The list of links reappeared and she half-heartedly scrolled down, used to fruitless evenings such as this. If they were out there, she'd find them. She'd lost hope long ago that they were looking for her in return.

Her sight blurry from fatigue she almost missed the link. Zachary Rogers. A short article in a Las Vegas newspaper about how he was working with at-risk young men by teaching them martial arts.

Her throat swelled shut with emotion and tears stung the back of her eyes. She had to take several deep breaths to keep from screaming out loud with a hope so strong it was painful. It's what she'd been living on for so long now and here it was. The first clue she had in a long time. The last one had brought her to Montana.

It might not even be her Zachary Rogers but it sounded like him. He'd always been the first person to reach out a helping hand. He would understand what those boys would be going through.

She quickly took down all the information from the newspaper article, her fingers shaking with excitement, her cheeks damp. Her chest tightened as she imagined a reunion. They'd hug and cry. He'd tell her about his life and she'd tell him about hers. How she'd never given up on him. The photo that went along with the story only showed some of the young men but not Zachary. It didn't matter how many years had gone by, she'd know him anywhere with only a glimpse.

Shoving the notes into her purse, she pulled out her battered wallet and paged to a photo in the middle of three children. The boy was the oldest and taller than the two girls although they were all small for their age. Gigi's mother had snapped that picture on one of her rare sober days. She'd taken them all to the park and bought them ice cream cones the remains of which could be seen smeared on their smiling faces. The sun had been shining and for that brief moment all had been right with the world.

It simply hadn't lasted. Nothing ever did.

But Gigi couldn't defeat the optimist deep inside and now she had a lead on her older brother's whereabouts. If she could find Zach, it would be one step closer to reclaiming her life. She'd never give up.

Chapter Four

GIGI POPPED A French fry in her mouth letting the salty flavor melt on her taste buds. It was another night on the campaign trail with West and tonight he was doing a Town Hall style meeting at the barbecue joint in Tremont. Lots of good food and mostly friendly people. There were a few potential voters that had shown up clearly to cause trouble and heckle West while he answered questions. More shenanigans by the current mayor but West didn't seem all that perturbed. He stayed calm and talked to the crowd until finally a few persons from the audience yelled the hecklers down.

She was glad to be here with West. After finding the possible link to her brother last night, she'd known her time in Tremont was coming to an end. This was it. Her last date with West. All along she'd planned to tell him when she was leaving but now that the moment was here she was too spineless to do it. He'd probably try and talk her out of it and when it came to him… She'd let herself care too much.

She'd write him a letter and say goodbye. It was the coward's way out but at this point she didn't feel like she had much of a choice.

"He's up ten points," Travis observed, settling into the seat next to her as West finished the last question. Residents of the town pressed forward to get a few minutes of personal conversation with the candidate. Luckily he seemed to take it all in stride, enjoying it. Gigi would have climbed up into the rafters to get away. She didn't like crowds or feeling hemmed in. "He's got a damn good chance at winning. We just need to keep the momentum going for the next three weeks."

"Mayor Cavendish might have something to say about that. Every day he's planting some smear story in the papers."

Today's tall tale was that West discriminated against women because there were no female detectives. It didn't matter that none had ever applied for the job.

"That man is a menace," Travis snorted. "He'll lie, cheat, and steal to get what he wants. Completely amoral."

Gigi had some experience with people like that.

"Yet he's been elected twice."

"Don't even get me started on voter apathy. If we can get the turnout we need, West will win by a landslide. If they don't show up, we're screwed."

Gigi let her gaze wander up and down West as he chatted with the owner of the grocery store on Main and Maple. Dressed in a dark blue suit, white shirt, and red tie he looked every inch the prosperous business man. In fact the only difference between the way he was dressed and his brother Travis was the color of the tie.

She hadn't realized when she started seeing West that his family was loaded. She'd heard about his reputation and prowess between the sheets but no one mentioned that the Andersons owned a good portion of Montana and part of Wyoming. When she'd found out it had made her slightly uncomfortable but she had quickly realized West was simply a regular guy. He played pool and darts, watched sports, and drank beer. He loved the outdoors and drove a truck. He was just like everyone else. Except he was gorgeous.

"I think he'll win. People seem really excited about his candidacy. I hear people talking about it at the diner every day."

Travis rubbed his chin and smiled. "I guess you would hear just about everything that goes on around this town. Is there anything that I need to know about me?"

Gigi had heard quite a bit about the oldest Anderson son. Mostly he dated women out of Tremont but the few that he had spoke of him with wistful sighs. An amazing lover, he was an intelligent and dynamic man who also had a daredevil streak. Few people wanted to go up against him whether it was in business or on the playing field. Travis Anderson was a winner and it oozed out of every pore.

"Someone told me you have a death wish," she teased. "I'm expecting you to ride a motorcycle and jump over a building or something."

Travis's grin widened showing off perfectly even white teeth. "I wouldn't mind trying but my reconstructed hip is reminding me that I'm over forty and should know better."

That explained the slight limp he walked with.

"Do you? Know better, I mean."

"Not really. I love the feeling of adrenaline I get when I jump from a plane or race a cycle. It's a rush you can't get just anywhere. Once you're addicted, I'm not sure you ever really get over it." He patted her shoulder. "But don't you worry about West. He's about as level-headed as they come. You won't find him bungee jumping off a mountain or fighting a bull in Spain."

No, she wouldn't have to worry about West. He'd be fine. He was that kind of guy.

"Are you flirting with my woman?" West's playful growl had Travis throwing back his head and laughing.

"I wasn't but it's not a bad idea. You shouldn't leave her all alone." Travis shook his finger at his younger brother. "It would serve you right if she left with me."

West reached down and wound his arm around her waist lifting her to her feet before pressing a long hot kiss to her lips. By the time he was done, her cheeks were flushed and her stomach all fluttery with butterflies. His potent brand of sex appeal was hell on her equilibrium.

"Ready? Sam packed us some barbecue to go. I say we go back to my place, turn on the game, and relax."

Relax was West Anderson-speak for have sex which was fine by her. One more night with him and she'd make sure it was a good one. Something to remember during the long, lonely evenings to come.

"I'm ready." Gigi linked her arm with West's, his body warm and strong next to her own. When she was with him she forgot to be scared. He had that alpha male vibe that made her feel protected and cared for. It was probably why she'd ended up being attracted to him when she'd turned down other guys who were just as good looking.

Okay…almost as good looking.

Waving goodbye to Travis, she and West strolled down the

mostly deserted sidewalk, the weather mild. Winter was around the corner and the flowers that had dotted the scenery had gone to sleep for their cold weather nap. She wouldn't be here in Tremont to see them wake up. Someday she wanted a home of her own with flowers in the front yard and a white picket fence. Maybe even a swing on the front porch where she and her husband could sit while their kids played in the front yard.

Gigi, you are dreaming. Why not imagine a puppy too while you're at it.

"You've been quiet tonight? Is anything wrong?" West asked as he unlocked the passenger side of his truck. "Are you tired of all this campaign stuff? I am too but it won't be much longer."

"It's fine," she assured him as he helped her climb into the truck and then handed her the yummy smelling bag of food. "I like going actually. I get to hear what's on people's minds and your ideas for making Tremont better. You're going to make a good mayor."

West swung into the driver's side and started the engine. "Now don't get too far ahead. I haven't won this thing yet. We still have three long weeks to go and a lot can happen in that amount of time. But thank you for saying that. I want to do a good job for this town. They deserve more than they've been getting."

"I like your idea about a teen center so kids have a place to go after school."

"That idea is going to be expensive, I'm afraid. I'm not sure how we're going to get it funded. I'm hoping for businesses to help out."

She rested her hand on his muscled thigh and could feel the

heat from his skin even through the heavy material of his trousers. "You're a very convincing guy. I'm sure you can get it done."

He glanced at her quickly before returning his gaze to the road. "If I'm so convincing how come I can't get you to admit you don't want to leave Tremont? I can see that you want to stay, babe."

That might have been true twenty-four hours ago but now she was anxious to get on the road and look into the lead she'd found. It would hurt to leave West, she could admit that to herself, but she wouldn't let that get in the way of locating and reconnecting with Zach.

She opened her mouth to tell West she was leaving in the morning but quickly changed her mind. This night was all she had left and she didn't want to spend it arguing and debating issues she'd already decided. She'd write him a long letter and explain…well, almost everything. Some things were better left unsaid.

"Can we leave that subject alone tonight? I just want to enjoy the evening."

"Sure we can let it drop. For now. But we're going to have to talk about this eventually. But I think spending the evening pursuing much more pleasurable activities does sound like more fun."

They didn't speak the rest of the drive to West's house. As they unpacked and ate their dinner, they kept the topics deliberately neutral neither one wanting to ruin the tenuous peace between them. When the meal was over, Gigi stood to clear the dishes but West also stood and reached, winding his arm around her waist and pulling her close.

"We can clear the table later."

His voice was husky and full of promises. Her body responded instantly knowing true pleasure was only moments away. No one made her feel like West did. He was a maestro in the bedroom knowing exactly how to play her erogenous zones for maximum effect, leaving her weak but sublimely happy.

Her nipples peaked under the cotton of her bra and a shiver ran up her spine as he slid his hand under her sweater to caress her midriff. A moan escaped from her lips as he nipped at the base of her throat while his fingers traveled upwards, unclipping her bra before cupping a straining breast in his rough palms.

He thrummed the hard point with his thumb until the ache ran straight to her slit and a bar of arousal had built in her abdomen. Gigi needed West. Desperately. Now. Knowing tonight was the last time made her voracious and needy, wanting him and only him. She might never feel this way again for the rest of her life.

At some point he'd backed her against the kitchen wall, her body smashed up against his, flattening her breasts. His lips had captured hers in a kiss that sent frissons of pleasure careening all the way to the tips of her fingers and toes before settling in her clit. Grinding her pelvis to his, she tangled her fingers in his dark, silky hair as he shoved up her sweater and bra before leaning down to lap at an already hard pink bud.

Gasping for air, she arched her back to give him more access. "Need you now. Don't make me wait."

Her own voice sounded tortured and gravelly but he understood the words perfectly. Tearing at the snap of her jeans, he pushed them down her legs until she was able to kick them away. His own breathing was labored and ragged, red streaks painting his cheekbones as he nipped and licked at a nipple. Her heart pounded out of control as she heard the sound of a zipper.

West lifted her until her legs were off the ground and her back was pressed firmly against the wall. "Are you ready for me, babe? Tell me you want it."

Gigi gritted her teeth and dug her nails into his scalp. "Give it to me, you asshole. Fuck me hard if you can."

Taunting an alpha male sexually was never a good idea but she loved it when Wes fucked her with a good head of steam going. Soft and gentle had its place but her favorite was when he completely dominated all her senses until her world narrowed to only the two of them.

West chuckled, his breath warm on her skin. "I'll give you exactly what you need."

In one swift stroke he drove in to the hilt, making her cry out with its beauty. So good. The sensation of being so completely filled was one she'd never get used to even if he fucked her every day for the next fifty years.

Her body pinned to the wall and her thighs spread wide, he initiated a fast, bruising rhythm that left her breathless and dizzy. The fire within built until she was being consumed in a white-hot inferno. Out of control, she clung to him her fingers digging into the muscles of his shoulders. Gasps, moans, and furtive whispers punctuated their frenzied coupling.

"Now, babe," he urged hoarsely, driving his length deep and hard until she tumbled over the precipice screaming his name as she fell. His came right after, his jaw snapped tight and a vein pulsing at his temple. They both drifted slowly back to earth still clinging to one another, a safe port in the storm.

Carefully he lowered her feet to the floor holding her until she could stand on shaky legs. He pressed a soft kiss to her lips so tender in comparison to their violent joining minutes before but then this man was a walking contradiction.

Swaggering alpha male one minute and gentle suitor the next. Was it any wonder she'd stayed so long?

Reaching down to the floor, he scooped up her discarded clothing in his hands and then gave her a wicked grin. "You are something else, babe. One of a kind."

She poked him in his chest with a finger. "I'm not done with you so don't rest on your laurels or start strutting around like the proverbial rooster. Meet me in the bedroom. It's going to be a bumpy night, officer."

West threw back his head and laughed, holding out her clothes. "Then I better get to it. How'd I get so lucky anyway?"

A swift pain ran through her heart like a sword slicing it in half. West was a lucky man. Loving family. Good job. Respect from friends and the town. He was the kind that would find someone else to love before too long.

It shouldn't have made her want to cry but for some reason it did.

Chapter Five

WHISTLING A HAPPY tune, West pushed open the door of the Tremont diner bringing a mountainous appetite with him. He and Gigi had made love into the wee hours of the morning and he definitely needed a hefty dose of protein, carbohydrates, and coffee.

Sliding into his usual booth only ten minutes later than normal, he waved to a few of the regular customers. The place was hopping but everyone knew the Head of Detectives ate in this booth at seven-thirty in the morning.

Karla, the owner, came over with a full coffee pot and began pouring him a cup. "Morning, West. The usual?"

Frowning, his gaze darted around the restaurant. "Where's Gigi? I thought she had a shift this morning?"

At least that's what she'd said when she'd crawled out of their warm bed at two this morning despite his protests.

"She did but she hasn't showed up. I tried calling her place but no answer. It's not like her. She's never even been late let alone taken a sick day or something. I hope she's okay."

Considering West had fucked Gigi's brains out for the better part of the night it was safe to say she was probably fine. Exhausted? Worn out? Sore, even? Yep. Sick? Not unless it had come on suddenly.

"I think I'll go check on her, Karla. Better make the coffee to go."

"That's a good idea. Let me get a cup for you." Karla bustled behind the counter and came back with a styrofoam cup and lid. "Let her know we can cover for her until she's feeling better. She's such a hard worker that I'm not surprised it all caught up to her eventually. She's managed to duck every germ around until now, poor thing."

"I'm supposed to meet Travis this morning. Let him know I'm checking on Gigi?"

"Sure will."

Bidding Karla a swift goodbye, West took his coffee and climbed into his truck, fear clawing at his empty stomach. Had Gigi come down with a cold or had she done what she'd been threatening since their first date?

Leave Tremont.

The thought that she could simply pack up without a word pissed him the hell off and his anger only grew as he drove the short distance to her apartment.

He'd work himself up into a righteous fury by the time he pulled into the parking lot and saw her standing by her sad little economy car. She was stuffing a battered suitcase into the hatchback and he didn't stop to think about the wisdom of his actions. He threw the truck into park and hopped out, stomping up so he was inches from her and looking down into her stricken gaze.

"West," she said faintly, as if she was shocked to see him here and didn't know what to say.

He pointed to her suitcase, his hand shaking slightly, struggling to keep a cap on his emotions. "Going somewhere? Karla said you didn't show up and didn't call. She thinks you're so sick you can't make it to a goddamn telephone."

Gigi's skin went pink and then turned pale, her throat bobbing as she swallowed hard. "I feel badly that I didn't call her. I hope you'll tell her I'm okay."

West wasn't going to tell Karla a thing. "If you want Karla to know something you'll need to tell her yourself. I'm not about to make this easier for you, babe. I just want to ask you one thing. One question. Did you ever give a single fuck about me or was this all just a game to you?"

Her lips trembled and her eyes were bright with tears, but her obvious remorse did nothing to assuage his anger. She'd been planning to leave without a damn word.

"Don't make this harder than it is—"

"Fuck that," West scoffed. "It doesn't look like very hard to me. You screw me all night long then grab a quick nap before packing your shit and hitting the road. Easy as pie from where I'm standing."

A tear rolled down her cheek and she brushed it away with the back of her hand. "I don't expect you to believe me but none of this has been easy least of all leaving today. But I have to go. I don't have any choice." She looked up at him and placed her hands on his chest. "And none of this was a game. I do...care about you, West. More than anyone in a very long time. But that doesn't change why I have to go. I'm so sorry."

West jerked away from her touch. "Bullshit. No one is running you out of town. You're leaving of your own free will and by God I want to know why. What's so scary that you have to run from town to town?"

He paced a few steps and then turned back so they were practically nose to nose, more tears dampening her cheeks now.

"Goddammit I've been patient, waiting for you to let me in but my patience has come to its end. I'm tired of the secrets, the subterfuge, and the avoidance of anything personal. I'm tired of playing the sweet, understanding suitor. You've pushed me too far, babe, and the bill has come due. You're going to march your sweet little ass back up those stairs and we're going to sit down. Then you're going to tell me what…in…the…hell…is…-going…on. Are you dying? Are you a CIA spy? Are you on the run from the law? What the fuck?"

Gigi buried her face in her hands, her shoulders shaking as more tears fell. This time West couldn't remain unaffected by the anguish pouring off of the woman he cared so deeply about. With a muttered oath, he hauled her into his arms and stroked her hair, speaking in soothing tones that everything was going to be alright.

Of course he had no idea if that was true but it sounded good right now. He let her cry it out for several minutes, his shirt front sodden. She hiccupped a few times and then pulled away slightly so she was looking up into his eyes.

"I'm sorry. I don't cry very often."

West hadn't known Gigi long but he had a feeling truer words were never spoken. "I think maybe those tears have been building for awhile, babe. Can we go upstairs now so you can tell me what's going on here and why you were leaving in secret?"

She hesitated for a moment and then nodded wearily. "Okay, but you won't change my mind. I really am going. I have to."

West slammed the hatchback on her vehicle closed. "Fine. Let's go upstairs. I haven't had near enough coffee for this."

They walked slowly back to Gigi's apartment and he settled her on the couch. There were a few boxes stacked up by the door that she hadn't had a chance to load into the car and he was once again slapped in the face by how few possessions she owned. He should have known she'd try something like this. Anger at himself clenched in his gut and he had to swallow against the acid that had crawled up into his throat.

"I'm going to make us some coffee and then you're going to tell me the truth. Finally."

She pointed to a box on the floor. "All the non-perishable food is packed up. I was going to drop it at my neighbor's door on the way out. The coffeemaker is in the other box."

Muttering under his breath, he retrieved the coffee and started a pot. The aroma of French roast beginning to fill the air in the small apartment. Leaving it to finish, he sat down across from her on the faded ottoman, his elbows on his knees, marshaling every ounce of patience he had. If he pushed too hard, she'd stubbornly clam up and that would just piss him off even more. They didn't need this conversation to go down that death spiral.

"So why were you leaving?"

Gigi's teeth sunk deeply into her bottom lip and her hands visibly shook. With fear? What did she have to be afraid of? Not him, surely?

"I–I can't stay. I'm looking for my brother and sister. I think I have a lead on Zach. He might be in Las Vegas so I'm going there."

It was the first personal thing she'd ever told him and he breathed easier that she hadn't tried to tell him a big fat lie. From her stormy expression it was clear she was being truthful, and it hurt.

"How did you come to be separated from your siblings?" He hoped asking a small question might prod more personal revelations but it also might backfire spectacularly.

"I don't want to talk about that."

West's gripped the edge of the ottoman careful to keep his tone even and controlled. "I understand that it might be painful to talk about. How about I ask another question? Is that why you've moved around so often? To find your siblings?"

More tears filled her eyes and she shook her head. "No...well...part of it. It's hard to explain."

"I've got all day. I'm not going anywhere."

Gigi twisted her fingers together so tightly the knuckles turned white. "I'm not sure I can tell you. I've never told anyone."

"I'm not just anyone, babe. And maybe it's time you told someone." He took a stab in the dark, terrified of the answer. "Are you wanted for a crime? Because if you are I can help you. I won't judge you, Gigi. You can tell me and I'll do whatever I can."

"Oh my God no." Her astonishment was real and he breathed a silent sigh of relief. "I'm not wanted by the police. I'm wanted by a man."

West leaned forward and captured her hands, holding them in his own. "What man? Who wants you?"

"Alan. Alan Morton. I can't let him find me. I won't let him." Her voice had gone up and he had to slide his hands up her arms to her shoulders to keep her focus on him.

"Then we won't let him. What does he want from you?"

West had been a cop for a damn long time and he'd heard enough statements from frightened women to be able to have an idea of what was coming next. A lump lodged in his throat making it hard to speak or breathe as she somehow found the courage to answer.

Gigi looked down at her worn tennis shoes before looking back up at him, real terror in those brown eyes.

"He wants me. And if he can't have me, he wants me dead."

Chapter Six

G IGI HAD SAID the words aloud.
The first time she ever had to another living being. She hadn't wanted to bring anyone else into the complete and total mess that was her life but West's confrontation had changed everything. Stubborn and…so damn bossy he'd got in her face and clearly wasn't leaving until he heard the entire story. For a moment she'd thought to lie but then there had been little point. He was on to her and being the detective that he was she doubted he'd give up before she bared her very soul.

"I think you'd better start from the beginning," West released her hands and came to sit next to her on the couch, the coffee forgotten. "Who is Alan Morton?"

She could answer that question but it wasn't the beginning of the story. "It all started long before I met Alan."

"When did it start?"

She stood and walked over to the living room windows and stared sightlessly outside, barely aware of the sunny autumn day. When she'd woke this morning after only a few hours' sleep the only thing she'd thought about was getting on the road and finding Zach. Now she was revealing secrets she'd planned to take to her grave.

"My mother had a drinking problem. A bad one. I don't have too many memories of her sober actually. The few that I do were wonderful but those days were few and far between."

She waited for his response. Revulsion? Pity? When he didn't say anything she continued.

"My older brother Zachary took care of us. Made sure we ate what little food was in the house and got us up in the morning for school. He was a stickler for brushing our teeth and washing behind our ears."

"We?" West prompted. "You have another brother or sister besides Zachary?"

"Aubrey. She's two years younger than I am. Zachary was five years older. I still remember the last time I saw them. It was the day my mother wrapped the car around a tree and died. Social Services came to get us and put us in foster care. I never saw them again. I asked every day and my foster family always said 'tomorrow.' But it never happened. As soon as I turned eighteen I started looking for them."

"Jesus, how old were you?" West came to stand behind her pulling her back against his strong frame. She couldn't allow herself the luxury of being weak though. She jerked out of his arms and went to the coffee pot, pouring two mugs.

"Eight. It wasn't like you're thinking. The foster family I finally ended up with was actually pretty nice. I have no horror stories of neglect or abuse. They just weren't my family and I was always aware of that. They'd had foster kids before me and they would have more when I left. They send Christmas cards though."

At least they had before she'd disappeared out of Chicago. The Warner family were lovely people and they'd done their best with a house full of dysfunctional children who often acted out their troubled psyches, but it had been more of a group home than anything. Gigi had fond memories of Karen and Stan but she'd never made the mistake of thinking they were mom and dad.

"What about your father?"

Gigi shrugged. "What about him? I've never met him and at this point I don't want to even if I knew where he was. My mother didn't have any other family, at least none that I know of. I assume the state would have tried to send us to them if they existed."

West's hands were wrapped around the mug, the knuckles white. Clearly he hadn't been exaggerating when he'd said he was at the end of his patience with her. But telling this story after so many years of keeping it hidden wasn't exactly easy.

"So you left your foster family when you turned eighteen. Is that how you met this Alan guy?"

"I didn't meet Alan for quite awhile. I was too busy trying to make ends meet. I worked every crappy job you can imagine from waitress, to hotel maid, to fast food clerk. They all sucked but they paid the bills. When I met Alan I was working nights as a cocktail waitress. He was there with some friends. I later found out they were his employees. He didn't have many friends and certainly no close ones."

"Employees? He ran a business?"

"A very successful business. He owns several nightclubs in the Chicago area."

"Sounds…glamorous, I guess. So then what?"

"He was charming. He asked me out and he treated me really well. He took me to fancy restaurants and bought me presents. I was overwhelmed honestly. No one had ever treated me that way. He swept me off of my feet."

Young, dumb, and impressionable, Gigi had fallen like a ton of bricks.

"But things changed?"

"I'd ignored all the red flags. He liked to choose my clothes and shoes. He wanted to know what my schedule was every day. He had to be in complete control at all times. I hadn't had anyone in my life pay that much attention to me. I thought that meant he loved me. It was only later that I saw it for what it was. He used to call me 'doll' and that's what he truly wanted. He wanted someone he could dress up and show off but then put back on a shelf for days or weeks at a time. He was constantly harping at me about my safety. He thought there was danger around every corner."

West slammed the mug down on the counter and began to pace the tiny space. "Did he hurt you? Tell me the truth, Gigi."

"Some hurts aren't physical."

The wounds that Alan had inflicted had been deeply psychological. It was only in the last two years that she'd been on her own that she could see him for what he was and what he'd done. He'd turned her into an emotional cripple dependent on his approval for every little thing.

"I'll still kill the bastard," West vowed, his hands curled into fists, his green eyes cold and flat. The man in front of her was a far cry from the playful, tender lover she'd seen up until now.

This man was the soldier turned cop underneath, stripped raw of his every day civilized veneer.

"He isn't worth your effort." She gripped the mug between her hands, the heat penetrating her cold fingers. "Alan wanted to control me and for a long time I allowed it. I was virtually a prisoner in his home. I couldn't leave unless he gave me permission. I was cut off from any friends. Anyone that could have pointed out what a fucked up relationship we had. For the longest time I thought it was normal."

West stopped in front of her, his fingers brushing against her cheek to tuck a stray strand of hair behind her ear. A gentle, caring gesture she'd never known until he'd come into her life.

"When did you figure out it wasn't?"

Just thinking about that day still made her shudder. Her knees weak, she sat down at the small kitchen table. The images still haunted her awake or asleep.

"Alan's employees would come over from time to time. I think he liked showing off for them. The house. The cars. That sort of thing. Anyway, one of the young men Stephen was very sweet and he and I talked for a long time that Saturday afternoon." She swallowed against the lump that had taken up residence in her throat. West must have felt her distress, placing his strong warm hands on her shoulders as if to give comfort. "When Alan found out he was furious. He had two of his employees hold Stephen while Alan punched him over and over until the man was covered in blood and he had to be carried out of the house. It was then I knew what Alan was capable of, and he wanted me to know. He made me stand there and watch a sick, twisted grin on his face when he was done. It was an unspoken threat and I took it seriously."

West's hands cupped her cheeks so she couldn't look away. "It wasn't your fault, babe. None of this is your fault."

"I shouldn't have been talking to him. I knew that Alan could be jealous. But it was just so nice talking to someone. I didn't realize how much I missed it."

Her voice shook and she blinked back the threatening tears. She was so damn sick of crying. It didn't change anything and only made her feel like crap.

"It's not your fault," West repeated. "It's this psycho Alan's fault. This is all on him. So how did you get away?"

"It wasn't easy. He made sure I didn't have much money. But one day he accidentally left some cash on his desk at home. He got a call and had to leave quickly so I guess he forgot about it in his rush. It was only two thousand dollars but I didn't hesitate. I shoved a few things in a backpack, grabbed the money, and ran to the nearest bus station. I took the first bus out of there which was headed to Kansas City. I've been looking over my shoulder every day since then."

West sat on the other kitchen chair, shaking his head. "Son of a bitch. It must have taken guts to leave like that. But I just have one last question."

"What's that?"

West slammed his fist down on the table making her jump and the surface shake. "Why in the hell didn't you tell me so I could help you? I'm a goddamn cop, babe. Why didn't you trust me enough to help you?"

His face was red with anger, his body practically vibrating as he tried to keep it in check. He was royally pissed off and she was the reason. She didn't blame him. He had a right to be and then some but it didn't make it easy to admit why she hadn't.

She buried her face in her hands but he wouldn't allow her to get away with not looking him in the eye. Gently, he tugged her arms away, his fingers tilting up her chin. She had to face how her decisions had made him feel.

"I couldn't trust anyone. Not after Alan. I'd trusted him in the beginning and it turned into a nightmare. When I left I decided that I wouldn't ever do that again and I've stuck to that. I know that you're different but somehow I still couldn't do it. I just couldn't. I don't know why."

She waited for his reaction and at first she didn't think she was going to get one. After a few moments he jumped to his feet and walked to the window as if he didn't trust himself near her.

"Gigi, I am so furious with you I don't even have the words to express myself."

The whole conversation had gone much better than she'd ever imagined. He hadn't walked straight out of the door and he was still speaking to her.

But it didn't change the facts. She had to leave. Telling West about her past didn't change the future.

Nothing did.

Chapter Seven

W EST FORCED HIMSELF to take a few deep breaths and count to ten. Livid with what he'd heard, he didn't know whether to spank Gigi or hold her close, kissing away her doubts and fears. Before this was all over, he'd probably do both.

"I understand why you're angry with me. I really do but I can't begin to describe my life these last few years. I'm afraid all the time. Every single day. And that doesn't set the stage for making great decisions."

That hurt. Deeply.

"You were afraid when you were with me? I'd never let anything happen to you, babe. I can't believe you don't know that."

"When I was with you I felt safe. Or as safe as I could be. But I couldn't be with you twenty-four hours a day could I? It wasn't your job to protect me anyway. That's my responsibility."

Things were about to change and his little Gigi didn't seem to have a clue.

"How's that working out for you?" He crossed his arms over his chest and stared down at the tiny woman who had disrupted his entire life. "Was this the plan? Run from town to town every few months for the rest of your life? And as for being with me twenty-four hours a day? Get used to it, babe, because you're not going anywhere. You have me and I'm going to put every resource I have available to me to solve this problem once and for all."

Gigi shook her head, her arms wrapped around her torso as if to ward off bodily injury. "I can't let you do that. I saw what Alan did to Stephen. I won't let him do that to you, or worse. That's just another reason why I have to leave Tremont."

She was cute when she was worried about him. "Do you think I give a rat's ass what this Alan guy thinks he can do to me? I don't think I'll lose any sleep about whether I can take him. Besides I don't plan to do this on my own."

"I don't want anyone else to get hurt," she said, desperation in her voice.

West was losing his patience again and had to rein in his temper. He'd never realized how stubborn Gigi could be when she'd set her mind to something.

"I'm going to protect you. I'm going to find this Alan and get him off your back. And I'm going to help you find your brother and sister. None of this is up for negotiation or discussion. We did things your way for three months. Now we're going to do it mine and see how things turn out."

If an expression could be happy, relieved, and pissed off all at the same time that's exactly how Gigi looked at the moment.

"You're bossy. Really, really bossy. I didn't realize that about you until today."

That was as close to acceptance as he was going to get. It would have to do.

"Then you've been lucky. According to my brothers, sister,

parents, and friends, I'm an ornery cuss who likes things my way as much as possible but then you and I were only doing the no strings relationship thing before. Oh, that's changed too, by the way. This relationship comes with lots of strings and complications. People throughout history have managed to make it work so I expect we will too."

"I can't make you any promises," she whispered, her gaze on the floor. "I don't know if I'm capable of what you would call a regular relationship with love and a future. I might be too screwed up."

He wanted to make sure she heard his words loud and clear so he knelt down again and looked into her watery eyes. She needed to believe in West down to her very bones.

"Then I'll make a promise. I promise to protect you with my own life. You don't ever have to be scared ever again. I will always be there for you."

She pressed her face into his chest and he heard a small sob as she wrapped her arms around his neck. "Now I'm scared for you."

It might be one of the nicest things she'd ever said to him. Because it spoke volumes about the feelings she didn't want to feel or talk about.

It gave him hope.

"Now tell me about the search for your siblings and what you've found. Then I'll call Jason and see if his firm can give us a hand with this."

✦   ✦   ✦

"I APPRECIATE YOUR help, bro. Gigi's been on the run way too long. We need to find this guy and fast. I'd be shocked if he's your basic law abiding citizen," West said, cradling his cell between his cheek and shoulder as he carried another of Gigi's boxes into his house. He hadn't taken no for an answer when he'd brought her home so he could keep an eye on her. She'd kicked up a fuss but he'd handled it fairly easily. She wanted to be with him, he could tell, but she kept believing she needed to be alone.

After her sleepless night, West had tucked her up in his bed and she'd been out in record time despite her protests that she wasn't tired and didn't need anyone to take care of her.

She needed it more than anyone he'd ever met. Clearly she'd been taking care of herself since she was a child and was used to it, and he respected the hell out of her for it. But that didn't mean she couldn't lean on him when the going was rough. It didn't make her weak but it didn't appear that she was convinced. She was going to fight him every step of the way. He'd have to be strong because eventually – and he didn't know when – Gigi wasn't going to be able to keep up this facade of having her life handled and under control.

"We shouldn't have any trouble finding him and what he's up to. I hate to ask this but how does Gigi know that Alan Morton is following her? Maybe when she left he gave up and moved on."

If only that were the case.

"He had his henchman follow her to the bus station and she barely got away. They also found her when she was in Nashville although luckily she was able to outrun them by ducking into a busy mall and getting lost in a crowd. Turns out they found her when she took a regular job instead the cash under the table places she'd worked before and since. Morton is a tech geek so if her name goes through a computer somewhere…he'll find her."

"He sounds like a sick bastard. I'm going to enjoy investigating this one. You're probably right about him. If he'll have a man beaten up for talking to a woman then crossing other legal boundaries probably isn't a big deal."

"That's what we need to be concerned about. If this asshole is as arrogant as he sounds he won't be thinking straight when it comes to Gigi."

"Arrogance and stupidity often go hand in hand," Jason chuckled. "He may be smart about business but that doesn't mean he's a genius when it comes to other subjects. If there's something to find we'll get him, don't worry."

"Gigi's worried about my safety." West slid the last box onto the dining room table. "She thinks Morton might hurt or kill me. It was real sweet."

"Brinley likes to worry over me too. It's a sign they care so appreciate it. Now, are you okay until the morning? I can come by and help out until Logan gets here. Jared's going to stay in Seattle and do the background research on Morton and the brother and sister unless you think I need to call him in as well."

"We'll be fine," West assured his brother. "I had her call into work and say she has the flu so she won't be expected for a few days. We'll be fine here in Tremont. There's no evidence that Morton knows where she is at this point. Then as soon as you and Jared get something concrete on Zachary Rogers we'll head out to find him."

"With Logan and myself shadowing you. I know you think

you can handle this guy with one hand tied behind your back but that doesn't mean you should do anything–"

Jesus, Jason was as bad as Gigi. Married life had turned him into a fussy old lady. "I get it. No running off by myself. We won't but just be warned. She's anxious to get on the road and find her brother. I practically had to wrestle her into bed to get some rest and give you a chance to confirm that the lead she has is legit. If she was running the show we'd be on the way to Las Vegas this very minute."

"First thing you need to learn is that when your woman ain't happy, you won't be happy," Jason laughed. "Let me get back to work then. Hopefully we'll have something for you by tonight, tomorrow morning at the latest."

"Thanks again. I mean that."

West had assured Gigi that he'd marshal every resource he could find to keep her safe and resolve the tangled mess of her life. He could do it by himself but it would be a hell of a lot easier – and faster – with Jason and his crew helping.

"Just keep an eye on your girl. Eventually she'll get used to the idea she doesn't have to be scared anymore."

West could only hope that would be the case and that when she wasn't terrified every day of her life she'd find a way to let someone in. Be vulnerable. Trust.

He wanted to be that man.

Chapter Eight

"ARE YOU HUNGRY?" West asked Gigi when she woke the next morning and wandered into the kitchen where he was tapping away at his laptop.

She looked deliciously rumpled and his first thought had been to take her immediately back to bed and stay there for the rest of the day. His second thought was that they still had too much to discuss. And the fact that he was still kind of pissed off that she'd been keeping this huge secret from him all this time. She hadn't trusted him in the least. "We could go get something to eat."

"I'm supposed to have the flu, remember? We have to stay in." Gigi yawned and stretched her arms over her head. The motion lifted her tank top, displaying a strip of skin that he knew felt like satin underneath his fingertips. Going back to bed was looking better and better with each passing minute. Damn, he was such a horndog around this little bit of woman. "I can cook breakfast."

"I won't argue. I got an email from Jason early this morning. He thinks the Zachary Rogers in Vegas has a good chance of being your brother. He moved there from right here in Montana where he was working on a ranch."

If West doubted Gigi's love for her brother or her determination to find him he wouldn't after seeing her blooming smile. She looked positively radiant. His chest tightened painfully at the thought of all she'd been through in her young life. He only wished he'd been around much sooner to make all of this go away.

Of course once she was free and safe there was no guarantee she was going to want to stick around a backwater town in Montana. To be honest he didn't know if they truly had any sort of future. He only knew what they'd had wasn't satisfying but what they could be wasn't clear yet. They were in some strange sort of limbo and it didn't feel comfortable. It wasn't the moment to talk about love but they'd gone past the casual stage. Basically it was put up or shut up time. They either moved forward together or went their separate ways. It would be hard but he had to be prepared for that eventuality.

"Then I was right when I followed his trail here?" Gigi asked excitedly. "I must have just missed him. I feel like I've been three steps behind him for years. Did they find anything on Aubrey?"

"No, but it's still early yet. Give them some time. They did find out quite a bit about your ex, though."

Gigi wrinkled her nose as she cracked eggs into a bowl. "Nothing pleasant I'm guessing."

"He's got his fingers in more than just nightclubs apparently. Did you know he did time before he met you? For assault. And the last few years he's been on the FBI's radar for possible RICO violations, money laundering and illegal gambling just to name a few. He has a bar on Division Street that they think is a front for a gambling den. Were you aware of it?"

"I worked there," Gigi replied with a grimace before pouring the egg mixture into a skillet and sliding bread slices into the toaster. "I tended bar a few nights a week in the beginning. I guess there could have been gambling going on. He had a private room upstairs for his VIPs but I never worked in it. After awhile he never let me go there at all."

"VIPs. Just another word for people with more money than morals." He'd already thought the guy was major slime even before Jason had called this morning.

"So when do we leave for Vegas? I don't want Zach to pick up and move on again before we can find him."

"Easy there." West held up his hand at her eagerness. Plans were still in progress. "We'll get there and we won't miss him. Now that we have an idea of who we think he is, we'll keep an eye on him. If he goes anywhere we'll be right behind him."

Gigi filled two plates with the scrambled eggs and toast. "I've waited so long to see him, I'm anxious. What are we waiting for? We could be on the road after breakfast."

Damn, the eggs were good. Gigi put some kind of spice in it that she'd brought from her apartment. West had been on his own for years and managed quite well but food always tasted better when someone else cooked it. "Not today. We're not just going to take off without a plan, a backup plan, and a backup backup plan. If Morton is after you my job is to make sure he doesn't come anywhere near us. That means preparation is key."

Grumbling under her breath, she half-heartedly dug into her breakfast. "You're being bossy again."

"That's probably only going to get worse before it gets better," West teased, finally getting a smile from his gorgeous breakfast companion. "I take this seriously, babe. Nothing and no one is going to hurt you ever again."

"You seem so sure. Alan told me that if he couldn't have me no one could. That means he doesn't just want to kill me. He wants to kill you too. That doesn't bother you?"

West placed both of their empty plates in the dishwasher. It was time for Gigi to see that he could handle what was ahead. It also wouldn't be a bad idea to teach her a few self-defense techniques.

Just in case.

"When I was in the Middle East there were thousands of people that wanted me dead so…no. It doesn't bother me. Or scare me." He dropped a kiss on her nose, catching a whiff of her shampoo. Vanilla and something else. Fresh and clean. He'd never smell that scent again without thinking of her. "If your tummy is full I have some plans for us today. And don't worry about anyone seeing us. We're heading to the ranch."

The Anderson family ranch was the perfect place to blow off some steam. She was tense and worried a state which wasn't going to go away on its own.

"The ranch? What for?"

"For a shooting lesson. Then maybe a fighting lesson. My dad never took down the boxing ring he built for us boys. You can work on your aggressions by beating the shit out of me. How does that sound?"

He didn't imagine how her eyes lit up and her smile widened. "I can't wait. But I warn you, I have a mean right hook."

West fervently hoped that was true. Before this was all over, she might need it.

✦   ✦   ✦

GIGI PULLED BACK her right arm and delivered a sharp upper cut to West's flat abdomen with her leather gloved hand, sending a shock wave all the way to her own shoulder. His torso had to be solid concrete. Instead of flinching or wincing, he'd grinned and danced around the ring before placing a soft tap to her chin as a reminder.

For the third time in the last ten minutes.

She kept dropping her arms. If she did this in a real fight she'd have a broken jaw or a black eye.

"Keep your hands up to protect your face, babe. Don't let me get a chance at it. Now try that kick again."

Faking a left hook, she kicked her right foot out in a kind of circle and connected with the heavy pad on the back of West's knee waiting for him to go down. He didn't budge.

"Do it again and harder this time," he urged with a grin. "Pretend I'm Alan."

Dancing round the ring on her tiptoes, she gathered all her strength and kicked as hard as she could, her instep landing with a thud against the padding. She grunted at the contact but raised her arms in victory adding in a rebel yell when West's knee almost hit the floor. He'd recovered quickly but if he hadn't been wearing those pads she could have really hurt him.

A rush of adrenaline ran through her and she punched at his solar plexus a few times before he – much to her frustration – tapped her on the chin again. She dropped her feet flat on the floor and stood still, groaning out loud in irritation. Covered in sticky sweat, Gigi had never been much of an athlete. She didn't like being dirty and she didn't like being uncomfortable. It wasn't a great combination for a woman who might need to defend herself against a violent asshole.

"What's wrong? You're doing great. That kick was epic. You almost had me down."

Bending over and resting her gloves on her knees, she gulped air into her starved lungs. "Almost doesn't count."

"It sure as hell does. Anytime you make it harder for your opponent to keep hurting you it's a win. Coming out of a physical altercation completely unscathed is not likely. You're trying to keep your injuries to a minimum while maximizing his so you can run away. All you're looking for is an opportunity to get away. That's it. You can't take him on toe to toe. You'll need to fight dirty and fast. He won't expect it."

"Let's hope I never have to use this."

"It's always good to know how to defend yourself. A couple of times a year I teach a course for women over at the Y." He pulled off his headgear and began to strip off the knee pads. "But I haven't taught you the most important move yet. Are you ready?"

Ready for two ibuprofen and a tall glass of iced tea. Fat chance.

West appeared to be serious about this. She stood up straight and nodded. "I'm ready."

"When an attacker comes for you, scream and scream loudly. Either yell 9-1-1 or 'fire.' Do not yell 'help.' You want people to come toward you not run away."

Was she supposed to shout now?

"Go ahead. Don't hold back. Give it to me as loud as you

can."

He'd asked for it. Gigi threw back her head and let out an eardrum busting, bloodcurdling scream. West jumped back a few steps before clapping his hands together in satisfaction. "That's exactly what I was talking about. You've got a hell of a set of lungs. I never dreamed you could do that. You always seem so quiet."

"Try being heard over a bunch of foster kids at the dinner table or when playing outside. If I wanted anyone to listen I had to make sure I was louder than everyone else. Practice makes perfect."

"It was like that at the Anderson dinner table too. Which reminds me, Mom invited us to lunch up at the house. After we eat, we'll go out to one of the empty pastures and practice shooting. Do you know anything about guns?"

"I may not be able to beat a man into the ground but I can shoot pretty well. I own a handgun and I know what to do with it. After I left Alan it was my number one priority."

West's brows shot up but he looked anything but convinced. "After lunch you can show me. Maybe I can give you a few tips."

Gigi wasn't so confident she didn't think she could improve. Learning from a real cop and a former soldier could only sharpen her skills. "Thanks, that sounds good." She pulled her damp t-shirt away from her body and grimaced. "I'm not sure I'm fit to be a guest in anyone's home though. I probably stink. No one wants that at their dinner table."

West began unlacing her gloves. "You can take a shower at the house. Leann has some clothes there that will probably fit you pretty well. Don't say no because Mom has her heart set on this."

Gigi liked West's parents very much but she'd always kept a certain distance between them knowing she would eventually be on her way.

"Do they know?"

"Only what they needed to know. You have a nasty ex and he's stalking you. They also know I'm helping you find your brother and sister. But I didn't get into the details."

She hoped she'd never have to tell them. It had been bad enough digging up all the skeletons for West without having to do it again. "I bet they wish you were dating someone else. Heck, anyone else."

She turned to head back to the truck but his arm stayed her movement. "Don't even go there. I love my parents but I'm a grown ass man and they don't get a vote as to who I'm with. If they don't like it – and I've seen no evidence that is the case – then they're just going to have to be unhappy. I stopped letting my mother pick my playmates when I was in the first grade."

His well-shaped lips were curved in a smile showing off that dimple in his cheek. "Playmate, huh? Is that what I am?"

He stepped forward so their bodies were only a millimeter apart. She could feel the heat from his skin and smell the tang of his after shave. Their gazes collided and sent a jolt of awareness all the way to her toes. "Among other things. I like playing with you. We have so many…games still waiting to be played."

Her breath caught in her throat, she could barely breathe let alone reply to his sexually charged statement. Seconds ticked away as they seemed drawn closer, his lips finally capturing hers, owning her senses in a kiss that left her clinging to him like a wilted vine. Her knees had given out and the only thing holding her upright was his strong arms wrapped snuggly around her waist.

Detective West Anderson was so damn sexy it ought to be illegal. If the cocky grin on his face was any indication he was well aware of it.

"We should get up to the house." Her voice sounded relatively normal despite the rhumba her heart was currently performing against her ribcage. "We don't want to keep your parents waiting."

"We've got plenty of time but this isn't the time or place for what I have in mind. Later."

His words held a world of promise and she couldn't control the release of butterflies in her stomach as he led her to the truck. It was hard enough dealing with her past but now she had a future to contend with as well.

Always before she'd left before any real feelings took hold inside but this time was totally different. West had grabbed a piece of her heart and wouldn't let go. She didn't want to care for him or love him, for heaven's sake. That would be a disaster. Foster kids from alcoholic mothers didn't fall for ranching royalty and expect a happy ending.

She simply wasn't sure she had any choice in the matter.

Chapter Nine

GIGI HADN'T BEEN lying earlier when she told him she could shoot. She'd easily knocked down the cans he'd set up on an old log way out in the far pasture. He'd tweaked a few issues with her stance and grip but all she really needed was more practice. If he'd known before that someone was out to find her he would have made sure she had the opportunity for target practice on a regular basis.

She'd also been charming at lunch and then again at dinner, entertaining his parents with stories of the eclectic diner clientele. He hadn't expected to stay this long at the ranch but after a long day it had been easier to let his mother cook dinner.

She'd made lasagna and that was one of his favorites. Plus chocolate cake for dessert. Heaven on a plate.

They were relaxing in the living room, practically the whole family there except for Leann. West knew his parents missed their only daughter but she wasn't fond of ranch life and the macho alpha males that seemed to populate it. Her last boyfriend had been some sort of artist – complete with a gold stud in his tongue – who liked to recite bad poetry.

Travis was filling in West's father on the recent restructuring in one of the business divisions while Brinley, Gigi, and his mother looked through old photo albums. West was pretty sure there were some pictures in there he wouldn't want a single soul to see but it was too late now. They were obviously enjoying themselves and their walk down the Anderson memory lane.

Jason nodded toward the kitchen. "Got a minute? I'd like to review the arrangements for tomorrow."

With a quick glance in Gigi's direction, West followed Jason into the other room. Gigi had been worried about getting along with his parents but she appeared to be fitting in just fine.

West settled into a chair at the kitchen table opposite Jason. "I really appreciate your help with this. I feel better knowing there's someone besides me watching over Gigi."

"Glad to help. Honestly the more I hear about Morton the more I dislike the guy. I talked to a friend at the FBI and he says the guy is ten kinds of dirty right along with his friends. But I can see how Gigi got caught up with him. His file says he's charming and well-educated. Likes museums, opera, and fine dining. That usually impresses the ladies."

"I just hope I get a chance to punch him right in the gut after everything he's put her through. Are you sure your friend doesn't have enough to arrest him yet? It would be much simpler if he went to jail."

"He's building his case. That's something we need to discuss after we find Gigi's brother and sister. My friend may be able to help with that as well. He's excellent at delivering messages I've found. At six-foot-four and two-hundred and fifty pounds, Faulkner stands out wherever he goes."

"Tell him I appreciate his help thus far. As for what to do

with Morton my goal is to put the fear of God into him. I want him to know that if he comes within a hundred mile radius of Gigi it will be very bad news for him. Painfully bad."

Jason rested his elbows on the table, his lips pursed in thought. "Listen, I know you want to beat on this guy for awhile and I can't say that I blame you a bit. But...you going to jail isn't going to keep your woman safe. You need to keep your head on straight and control your temper at all times. I think we can scare Morton off just using the information we already know. He doesn't want any more attention from government authorities than he has already."

The terrified expression Gigi had worn when she told her story still haunted West. That she'd lived with fear that great every day for so long made him want to wrap her in cotton wool and keep her safe for the rest of her life. "When you put it like that I'd settle for one good punch."

Jason laughed and shook his head. "Don't do anything stupid, little brother. Alan Morton is one bad dude who doesn't give a shit. So what if you put a hurt on him? He's got a dozen henchmen to come after you and mess up your pretty face. And let's be honest here, your looks are about all you have going for you."

"You're an asshole, big brother," West smirked. "You're just jealous of my brains and talent catching those bad guys."

"I think I'll hobble through life just fine. Now let's talk about tomorrow. If we get on the road early, before sunrise, it would be best. I'll be in the lead, you and Gigi in the middle, and Travis bringing up the rear. We need to keep in constant radio contact and stick closely together no matter what."

"Travis? I thought Logan was driving in today to do this?"

"The twins both have the flu," Jason sighed. "He and Ava have their hands full. Travis kindly offered to help out but it tells me that I need to hire another field man."

West stood and paced the kitchen, too restless to keep still. He was anxious to get on the road, find Gigi's siblings, and then put an end to Morton reign of terror. But he was a cautious man and one thought kept running around in his brain.

"What if this guy really brings it? If what Gigi says is true – and I don't have any reason to believe it's not – he wants her and he doesn't care what he has to do to get her. He's got badass men to do his bidding. And money. Which tells me he can buy even more people to do his dirty work. What if he sends an army? Are we prepared?"

Jason didn't laugh or scoff at the question. "Your job is to keep Gigi safe. Always remember that. If we get ambushed, you get her and run. Don't worry about us, we can take care of ourselves. We'll be loaded for bear and ready and willing to do what needs to be done."

West rubbed his throbbing temple. He hated the waiting around and was as anxious as Gigi to get this show on the road. "If anything happened to her…"

"Love's a bitch but what's a man to do when he's found the right one? You can tell your kids the story in twenty years."

Sitting straight up, West shook his head in denial. Marriage talk made him nervous. Jason was way off the mark here. "We're not in love. It's not like that."

"Sure. Right. Whatever you say. Except that you two both look like you're in love. I could be completely wrong. But I doubt it."

Clearly Jason was laughing at West but the situation wasn't funny in the least. Love was not in the equation here. West cared about Gigi but wasn't ready to call it anything more. She sure as shit wasn't in love with him. She'd been packed and ready to leave his ass in the dust without a backward glance.

"I don't want to talk about my fucking feelings."

Jason raised his brows at West's tone. "That's fine with me but don't think because you don't acknowledge them they'll just go away. I can personally attest to that."

"What time will you be at the house tomorrow?" West changed the subject heartily tired of the last one. He wasn't a touchy-feely kind of guy who wanted to talk about love, rainbows, and unicorns.

"Five. Brinley offered to make us breakfast and pack it for the road plus some snacks so hopefully we can put a few hundred miles behind us before we have to stop. Be ready when we get there."

West was more than ready. Finding Zachary Rogers and reuniting him with Gigi was the first step in getting back her life.

Alan Morton would be the second.

GIGI HAD TROUBLE keeping her eyes open, her lids weighted down with fatigue. After the physical exertion of today, she was wrecked. She'd be out like a light as soon as her head hit the pillow which was really a shame. There had been some serious sexual tension between her and West earlier and this might be the last night they had alone for awhile. But she wouldn't complain. For the first time in forever, Gigi felt safe. Or safer. She'd almost forgotten how wonderful it felt.

The streetlights whizzed by as West drove them back to his house to finish packing and get some rest before their road trip tomorrow. She'd wanted to fly to Vegas but all three Anderson men had quickly squashed the idea. Jason especially had shaken his head and said that if Morton knew anything about computers he was probably monitoring transportation databases looking for her name. Then he'd grinned and excused himself to call someone named Jared about planting a false record to send Morton off the trail.

These men didn't miss a trick and for that she was immensely grateful.

By the time he pulled into his driveway, she was half asleep, dozing on and off. "Home sweet home, babe. Next stop, dreamland. I'll have you in bed within ten minutes."

"Promises, promises," she giggled with a wide yawn, rubbing her eyes. "You've never had much trouble getting me in bed, that's for sure."

West gave her a lopsided grin. "You weren't easy. I remember being nervous as hell on our first date because you acted like you didn't care one way or another if you were there or not. I was sweating."

"It was picnic in July. We were all sweating."

She remembered that sunny and hot day well. They'd eaten fried chicken and apple pie next to the lake and then took a ride on his Harley. He'd kissed her goodnight under a new moon and she'd never been the same since. He'd slowly become the best thing in her life.

He helped her out of the truck, handing her the chocolate cake his mother had wrapped up for them so he could carry the gun case and range bag that held the firearms and ammunition they'd used earlier. When they were inside he set the case and the bag on the coffee table before pointing up the stairs. "Go on up. I need to do a few things and then I'll join you."

No way was she going to argue. She was dead on her feet, barely remembering to place the chocolate cake in the refrigerator. "Don't be too late. You need your sleep too."

"Thirty minutes tops. Fifteen if I'm lucky. But I doubt you'll be awake that long."

She wasn't too tired to get a goodnight kiss. If she wasn't going to get lucky at least she'd get some sugar from this gorgeous hunk. Looping her arms around his neck she gave him her best come hither look. "How about a kiss for sweet dreams?"

His rough fingers caressed her cheek, sending a shiver of awareness down her spine and straight to more personal parts. Two muscular arms lifted her until she pressed against him, her legs wrapped around his lean middle. "Sweet dreams, huh? That doesn't sound like any fun. How about hot dreams?"

She wasn't feeling all that exhausted anymore. Blood fizzed in her veins like champagne while flames licked at her flesh, sending arrows of pleasure through her body. In this mood West was devilishly lethal.

"You might have to help me with that," she whispered, her lips caressing his stubbly jaw while his hands roamed over the curve of her bottom. "Hot sounds good."

So very good. His mouth took control of their kiss, dominant and playful at the same time. She gave herself over to him,

OLIVIA JAYMES

happily following his lead until they were both breathless and aroused. She moaned as his lips traveled over her jaw to nibble at her earlobe before sliding down to a shoulder, her heart galloping a mile a minute.

"Let's go upstairs," she urged, letting her head fall back to give him unfettered access to the nape of her neck.

Instead of nibbling at her sensitized skin he took a step back, his expression conflicted. "You know I want to, babe, but you're dead on your feet and we need to be on the road early in the morning. I've still got a few things I need to take care of. If I carry you up those stairs neither one of us is going to get any sleep for quite a while."

"Suddenly I'm not very tired," she teased, running her hands up and down his muscled arms, the flesh warm under her palms.

He captured her hands in his and pressed a kiss to her knuckles. "I take this seriously. You've been scared for too long. I want to give you some peace of mind if I can and to do that I need to make sure I don't lose focus. There are things that need to be done before we leave in the morning."

She admired his dedication but damn if she wasn't more than a little disappointed too. West could rev her engine with a simple kiss but she'd waited for a man like this for a long time. Someone who put her safety and well-being before his libido.

Crap and double crap. She'd fallen for an honorable man and this was the result. Safe. Sound. And aroused.

"You're a good man, Westin Anderson." She pushed at his shoulder playfully. "A frustrating one, but good. You get me all wound up and then…nothing. A girl could get a complex, you know."

He tugged her back into his arms, the warmth from his body easily penetrating her blue jeans and shirt to heat her skin. "I'll promise you here and now that when we get to Las Vegas the odds will definitely be in your favor. In fact, let's call it two-to-one. Two orgasms for you for every one of mine. Deal?"

She liked those odds.

"Deal." She stood on tiptoe and kissed his cheek. "Seriously, don't stay up too late. You need to sleep as much as I do."

He gave her bottom a playful slap as she passed him on the way to the stairs. "Just don't hog the covers. It's supposed to be cool tonight."

Bounding up the stairs, Gigi felt more hope than she had in a long time. She'd told the truth to West and he was determined to keep her safe and help her find her siblings. Plus the Feds were looking into Alan's dealings in Chicago.

Maybe she had a future after all.

Chapter Ten

GIGI WAS HAVING a wonderful dream.

She and West were walking hand in hand down a white sandy beach, cool water lapping at her toes and the warm sun beating down on her bare skin. Birds glided overhead while palm trees swayed in the gentle breeze. The scent of coconut oil and hibiscus filled the air and she kicked out her foot playfully, splashing water on West's legs. He laughed and pulled her closer, a wide grin on his handsome face. Leaning down to look into her eyes, he cupped her cheeks in his strong hands, his face inches from her own as if to tell her something very important.

"Don't say anything."

Gigi sucked in a breath, her eyes flying open.

Her heart raced and her body trembled at being awoken so abruptly. West sat on the edge of the mattress, his fingers pressed to her lips. She opened her mouth to speak but he shook his head. Instead of talking he tossed the covers aside and drew her out of bed. Guiding her to the large walk-in closet in the corner of the room, he opened the door and backed her into it, pressing a handgun and a flashlight into her shaking fingers.

"There's someone trying to break into the house. They're

trying all the doors and windows. Stay here while I take care of this and don't come out for anything. Nothing, do you hear me? When I'm done I'll knock on the door three times. Got it?"

She heard him although he'd kept his voice deliberately soft and low. Taking a deep breath to calm her nerves she grabbed onto his arm, not wanting him to go out there.

"It's dangerous. Call 911."

The minute the words were out of her mouth she realized how idiotic they sounded. West was the police and handling a burglar was probably a boring night for him.

"Obviously you haven't woken up yet, babe. I've got this. Just stay here and be safe. I'll be fine. I've already called for backup."

Of course he would have. He was a trained cop and she was still bleary-eyed from REM sleep. Just for a little extra added embarrassment her hair was probably sticking straight up as well.

"Can I help?"

"Yes. You can help by not doing anything that would distract me. So stay here until I come and get you. If anyone doesn't knock and tries to come through that door? Shoot them."

Instructions didn't come much clearer than those. She nodded and he closed the closet door behind him, leaving her in the dark. She took a few steps backwards until she could feel hanging clothes on her back. Sinking to the floor, she leaned back on a cardboard box, squirming to try and get comfortable.

Her heart had slowed to its normal pace and she stretched her legs out from their cramped position. There was nothing to be afraid of, really. West would catch the burglar and she'd sit here like a fool in the closet with a loaded gun.

Kind of ironic. She'd been waiting all these months for one of Alan's men to come for her but tonight she was cowering in a closet because of someone who wanted to steal West's Xbox.

Life was strange.

✦　✦　✦

WITH ALL THAT was going on in West's life the last thing he needed right now was to fend off a burglar. Probably some young kid or maybe a junkie looking to score a DVD player, iPhone, or a Playstation that would bring a quick buck. He should be lying in bed next to Gigi catching up on his sleep but instead he was climbing out of his bedroom window and walking as silently as possible on his roof.

Dropping to his knees, he slowly crawled close to the edge that hung over the side of the house. Coming from the ground below, he could hear a few whispers and the sound of someone shaking the window frame.

West craned his neck and was able to make out two figures in the shadows. Not the best odds but then he'd been in much worse. If the guys were amateurs they'd run the minute he identified himself.

Easing the .38 from his shoulder holster he pointed the barrel down at the dark outlines before shouting. "Police! Drop any weapons and lie on the ground."

Normally that command – out of the blue and in the middle of the night – was enough to get a perp to piss himself before he went belly first into the grass shouting he was innocent and it was all a set up. Or he called for his lawyer.

It didn't matter which to West. The guy could tell it to the judge at arraignment the next morning.

This time neither of the figures did any of those things. West barely had time to scoot back and duck his head as one raised his arm in West's direction. There was a flash of light from a gun barrel piercing the darkness and then he felt the whistle of a bullet fly past his ear. Flattening his body to the rough shingles, he heard three more shots ring out in his general direction but none as close as the first.

What the fuck?

An urgent unintelligible whisper and then the thud of footsteps in the grass as the men ran, probably toward a getaway vehicle. West swung down from the roof, landing with a jolt on the air conditioning unit before jumping to the ground. Glad he kept himself in excellent shape he broke into a sprint, the men not far in front of him.

"This is the police! Stop!" he bellowed again but he already knew they weren't going to stop fleeing the scene. If they had the audacity to shoot at a police officer they weren't going to suddenly throw down their weapons and surrender like good little citizens. The sound of sirens in the distance indicated however that backup would be there momentarily and West could get this situation under control. This was a residential neighborhood and West didn't want any of his neighbors to get hurt.

Especially not the woman who was hopefully following his exact instructions.

One of the men looked over his shoulder and wildly fired two more rounds, one hitting a window in West's house and the other flying off into the air. These assholes were going to hurt an innocent bystander at this rate and already lights were coming on in windows down the street, one by one. Soon people would be streaming out of their houses and into the line of fire, drawn by the sound of shots.

Stay where you are, babe. Just stay there.

West raised his gun but one of the men dashed into the darkened street as the police backup careened into the neighborhood, sirens blaring and lights flashing. Whether the perp was temporarily blinded or simply not paying attention West didn't know, but the man bolted straight into the path of the oncoming vehicle. There was a squeal of tires and the sickening sound of metal on bone. West's stomach twisted in his gut and he winced at the splash of red on the black and white cruiser.

Bodies streamed from the homes along the street and West lost sight of the other man until he heard the roar of an engine and a vehicle barreling out of the neighborhood. He couldn't make out the license plate but he could tell it was a dark Ford Escape, possibly navy blue or black. Pulling his phone out of his pocket, he quickly sent a text to Nancy who was working police dispatch tonight about the speeding SUV. He added, "Armed and dangerous. Do not engage without backup."

With more sirens screaming in the background West knelt next to the injured man. The other officer had already started administering first aid and West was careful to stay out of the way while still getting a glimpse of the suspect's face.

Shit. No one he knew.

Strange that someone from out of the area would be breaking into homes but the economy wasn't the greatest and desperation made people do strange things. Another cop car pulled into West's driveway and Lou Blanton hopped out. Lou was an experienced officer and a good man to have on the scene.

I need to get to Gigi.

"Jesus, you take a leave of absence and this is what happens?" Lou peered down at the blood covered man and grimaced. "What's going on here?"

West stood and pointed back to his home. "Two guys trying to break in. Heard them trying the doors and windows. I gave them the usual warning and told them to stop but they started firing on me before taking flight. I pursued and they continued to fire on me but this one ran into the path of Jerry's cruiser. The other got away in a dark SUV. Late model. I asked Nancy to put out a BOLO."

Lou whistled and jotted down a few notes. "Did you discharge your weapon? Damn, there are too many people around here. We'll need a couple of officers just to deal with the crowd."

More officers were arriving along with an ambulance, the flashing lights illuminating the entire block. For a measly burglary attempt this was quite a mess. The local news was bound to show up any minute.

"No. Too many people. I never had a clear shot." West paced, too wired to stay still. "Listen, I have someone in the house and I need to give them the all clear. Can you handle this?"

Lou was more than capable and West needed to get back to Gigi, who had to be on pins and needles listening to the gunfire and wondering what was going on.

"Sure. It looks pretty routine. Foiled attempted burglary with an added injury when the suspect ran. Jerry looks pretty shook up though."

The young cop who had been first on the scene was pale and standing a few feet away from the prone man while the EMTs worked. The stricken expression of the officer told West that he needed to make sure that he talked to the kid. Jerry hadn't done anything wrong but he was clearly blaming himself.

"I'll be back in a few."

West slapped Lou on the back and jogged into the house and up the stairs. He almost pulled the door open but then remembered he needed to knock first. He could have been the recipient of a lead bullet in the chest. His woman was a damn good shot.

"Gigi? It's me, babe. You can come out now."

The door cracked open slowly and she peered around it. Obviously shaken, her hands trembled and her skin had a gray cast to it as she held out the firearm. "I heard gunfire. Are you okay?"

The minute he took the gun her hands ran over his arms and chest, her gaze darting from head to toe. He shook his head and placed the firearm on the chest of drawers before tugging her close. He could feel the her heart race and her body quiver so he simply held her for a long time, stroking her hair and whispering that everything was going to be okay.

"I'm fine, babe. It's all fine. They never got in. Not even close. They just didn't like it when I interrupted them, that's all. It's all fine."

She pressed her cheek to his chest and he rubbed his chin on the top of her head, the vanilla scent of her shampoo wrapping around him. "Are you hurt? Are you okay? Did you get them? Are they going to jail?"

Shit. No. "One is headed to the hospital. He ran into the

path of the police car. The other took off but we're looking for him. We'll get him."

If not tonight then one in the future. The guy didn't appear to be an amateur. If he did this for a living West would be meeting up with him eventually.

"What happens now?" Gigi's voice quivered and his heart twisted at her anguished tone. She'd been frightened, worried about his ugly ass, which was sweet. It kind of gave him hope that maybe she cared a little. Or a lot.

"Grab your toothbrush and we'll go spend the night at Travis's house. This is a crime scene technically and we both need some sleep."

Travis had a big house on the ranch and he wouldn't mind being woken in the middle of the night. In all probability the workaholic was awake and staring at the screen of his laptop while drinking a beer.

It only took a moment for Gigi to pull on a pair of blue jeans and grab a toothbrush, stuffing it into her purse. West gave Travis a quick call to let him know they were coming and that he'd get all the details when they arrived. By the time West locked the front door he was ready to put this night behind him. A complete cluster.

"Do you need anything else from me, Lou?" West asked, one arm around Gigi as they stood outside. Most of his neighbors had become bored and gone back to bed except for a few stragglers here and there. Jerry was still standing where West had left him, watching the EMTs lift the suspect from the ground and onto the gurney.

"We're good. But I'm guessing the chief is going to want you to file your own report."

They were supposed to get on the road in a few hours but that plan was blown all to hell. But he wouldn't leave Gigi right now when she was so scared. There would be time enough for police procedure in the morning.

"You're probably right. I'll come by tomorrow. There's not much to tell."

The EMTs were rolling the gurney toward the ambulance and West held out his arm to stop them for a moment. "Is he going to make it?"

The man's forehead was covered in blood along with several cuts on his arms and he appeared to be unconscious. They'd stabilized him with a neck brace and a backboard in case he had more serious injuries.

"I think so," the taller EMT assured West. "Although he took a hell of a knock to the head. He's probably going to need surgery for that leg too."

Gigi came up beside West and placed her hand on his arm. She'd calmed down, the color back in her face.

"Is he dead?" she whispered.

"No. He'll be okay. Eventually."

Gigi peered down at the man and West heard her quickly indrawn breath. She must be squeamish about blood and guts.

"Why don't you wait for me in the truck?"

Her fingers dug into his arm, the nails scoring his flesh painfully. "I know him."

"You've seen him in the diner or around town?"

Gigi might be able to help them identify the one that got away as well. Maybe things were looking up after all.

"No." Her voice was choked and she looked up at him, a tortured expression across her pretty features. "I know him from Chicago. He works for Alan."

Her knees seemed to buckle at that moment and he had to catch her to keep from sprawling on the grass. Tears were falling down her cheeks and she fisted his shirt in her hands and buried her face in his chest.

"Oh God. He's found me. I have to get out of here right now. Tonight. I can't stay."

That wasn't an option but getting her to safety was now his top priority. How this Alan asshole had found her West didn't know, but he wouldn't let this guy within five miles of Gigi. The fucker would have to go through West's cold dead body.

"I'm not going to let anything happen to you. You're safe with me. He didn't get to you earlier and no one is going to get to you tonight or any other night. Do you hear me, Gigi?"

She nodded, rubbing her cheek on the damp cotton of his shirt but she didn't speak, her trembling body communicating her terror better than any words could have.

If Alan Morton wanted to come after Gigi then it was game on. West had planned to deal with this sick bastard after they found her siblings but some things wouldn't wait.

Alan had been moved to the top of West's shit list. A place no one wanted to be.

Chapter Eleven

"CAN I GET you something to drink, Gigi?" Travis asked as he led her into his house. "Coffee? Hot chocolate? Shot of whiskey?"

After the shock of seeing Frank on that stretcher West had bundled her up with a blanket around her shoulders and placed her in his SUV until Travis showed up. With her news West couldn't leave the scene and even Jason Anderson had been dragged from a warm bed to help out.

Her life had looked like it was going in the right direction and then everything had exploded.

"Actually a shot of whiskey sounds like a good idea," she said, pulling the blanket around her more closely. A welcome numbness had invaded her bones as she'd shed tears on West's shirt. Crying didn't help the situation and only made her look weak. She wasn't fucking weak. She'd survived this long and she'd keep on doing it. She was only sorry that West and his brothers had placed themselves in the line of fire.

"Have a seat and relax. I'll get us a couple of drinks and you can tell me what's going on and how I can help."

Travis Anderson was a nice man. Not every brother would

have welcomed a call in the middle of the night asking him to come to a crime scene and pick up his little brother's girlfriend. West had planned on driving her to Travis's home himself but after her revelation he'd had to change plans.

So Travis had nicely agreed to come pick her up.

"Here you go." Travis smiled and handed her a highball glass with a shot of amber colored liquid. Knowing the Anderson family this would be an excellent single malt scotch.

"You have a beautiful home." Delaying the inevitable discussion, Gigi tried to make small talk. It was a beautiful house though. Large and airy, its understated elegance spoke of a man with good taste and ample resources. Travis Anderson obviously liked quality and enjoyed being comfortable, whether it was the butter soft leather couches or the huge flat screen television that hung over the fireplace taking up half the wall. "I've never seen a television that big. Does West know that it exists?"

Travis chuckled and sat down in a chair to her right. "He does. I bought it right after he purchased his television."

The three Anderson brothers were quite competitive but she hadn't realized just how much. But then her brother Zach had always enjoyed the challenge of sports and academics, although he'd never tried to compete with her or Aubrey.

"I guess we won't be leaving for Vegas in the morning," she sighed, sipping the whiskey and feeling the heat all the way to her belly.

"Is that your biggest concern?" Travis idly twirled the glass on the coffee table. "If you hadn't been at a cop's house tonight someone might have tried to kidnap you…and succeeded."

Her fingers tightened on her own glass at the thought of being under Alan's control. His prisoner. She'd never allow that to happen again. Some things were worth dying for and freedom was one of them.

"I wouldn't have gone quietly."

"I have no doubt you would have made it as difficult as possible for them but there were two men and one of you."

Travis didn't sound derisive or flippant. His tone was conversational, as if they were discussing the weather or the price of milk.

"I'm anxious to get to Vegas and reunite with my brother. And then find my sister, of course." Gigi changed the subject away from her would-be captors. She was still trying to wrap her mind around Alan tracking her down after all this time. All the running and hiding. She'd messed up somewhere along the line but she didn't know how, what she'd done wrong.

"West says you haven't seen them since you were a little girl."

"Yes, but we were very close as children. Zach sort of took care of me and Aubrey. As much as he could anyway."

"He sounds like a good guy. He's older than you?"

An image came unbidden into her mind of the budding young man he'd been the last time she'd seen him. He'd rarely smiled, always serious. But then he'd had to be. Taking care of two little girls wasn't a job for a little boy but he'd never shirked away from the responsibility.

"Five years older. He was the best brother a girl could ask for. I always felt badly that he could never just be a kid like the other boys. He had us to take care of."

Travis's expression softened. "I have a little sister so I know how precious they are. I'm sure he was happy to do it even if there were times he'd rather be young and just have fun. Have you had any luck finding your sister?"

"No. It's like she's disappeared. She's two years younger than me so when I turned eighteen I looked for her in the foster system but no luck. I haven't had any sort of lead all these years."

Gigi's greatest fear and one she'd never spoken aloud was that Aubrey was dead. But she'd never found a death certificate so she still held hope in her heart that her little sister was alive and well. Somewhere.

"Tell me about her," Travis invited, stretching out his long legs and relaxing back against the overstuffed cushions. "Were you and she alike?"

Gigi took another sip and let the liquor slide down her throat before answering. "Not in the least. Physically or any other way. She has dark hair and eyes but the real difference is that Aubrey is so creative. She was always singing and dancing around the house. I used to tell her she was going to be a star when she grew up. She's also very quiet and shy. It was hard for her to meet new people so she looked to me to navigate her way through new situations. That's why I always worried about her when we were separated in foster care. That had to be hard on her. She must have been so frightened."

Travis regarded her steadily over the rim of his glass. "You're a good sister, Gigi. I don't know where Aubrey is but I'm sure she remembers how you took care of her. I bet she's trying to find you too."

Tears burned the back of her eyes and she blinked several times, determined not to give in to them. "She won't be able to find me. After Alan I went underground. I live completely on cash and I don't even have an email address that can be linked back to me. That's what so crazy about this whole night. How did Alan find me this time? I'm so careful."

Travis grimaced and rose from his chair, walking over to a desk tucked in the corner of the room. "I think I might be able to shed some light on that. When West called me earlier I couldn't imagine how your ex found you either but then I remembered this." Travis opened his laptop and tapped on the keys before bringing it over to the coffee table. "A national news site picked up the local article on the debate between West and Cavendish. It was the usual political bullshit characterizing my brother as some rich spoiled brat born with a silver spoon up his ass, completely ignoring the fact that we grew up in a two bedroom home for most of our childhoods."

"What does that have to do with Alan finding me?"

Gigi remembered the article in the paper by a reporter who they suspected was on Cavendish's payroll.

Travis pointed to the screen. "They also picked up the photo that was in the paper. A photo of you and West."

Stiffening at the sight of herself and West smiling up at one another, she groaned and buried her head in her hands. It was a photo that was sure to stoke Alan's most possessive instincts. He surely wanted to hurt if not kill West and possibly her as well. He'd been extremely clear that day that he'd beat Stephen within an inch of his life.

If I can't have you, no one will. You belong to me, Georgette. I own you, and I'll do as I please with you. I can give…and I can take away. It's up to you which way I go. Keeping you safe is my priority.

Shuddering with remembrance, she could feel Travis's probing gaze on her face. She'd long ago stopped hiding her revulsion toward Alan so she was sure it was plainly visible in her expression tonight. She wouldn't allow him to touch her ever again.

"He hurt you." It wasn't phrased as a question so perhaps he didn't expect a reply.

"He never hit me."

"Did he force himself on you?"

She could hear the suppressed violence in Travis's tone and she reached over to pat him on the hand, not wanting his imagination to make things worse than they were. They were bad enough without adding to them.

"No." She shook her head, not sure how to explain the sick relationship she'd had with Alan toward the end of her time with him. "When I started pulling away from him he allowed it. Gave me my own room. It wasn't about sex with him. It was about ownership. He wanted to possess me completely. My thoughts. My emotions. Everything. The physical side wasn't important to him as long as I wasn't having sex with anyone else. He didn't even want me talking to anyone but him. That last year I was mostly in isolation in my room."

Travis's hands were balled into fists and a muscle ticked in his jaw. "Morton sounds like a sick man. I think I'm going to enjoy helping send him to prison. Guys like him should be behind bars and away from society. Rehabilitation isn't in the cards for a man like him."

She drained the last of the whiskey and placed the glass on the table next to the laptop. "I just want him to leave me alone so I can live my life in peace."

"That's the plan. Does that life include my brother by any chance?"

A smile played around Travis's lips and warmth flooded her cheeks. "I think it's too soon to be talking like that. He and I haven't been dating long and we've been keeping it very casual."

Travis snorted, his shoulders shaking with laughter. "Casual. Sure. That's why he's growled at any man that dares come within a few feet of you or even – heaven forbid – smile at you. That's casual, alright. I'd hate to see how he acts if you two were serious."

"I won't be tied down," she said stubbornly. "I've wasted too many years either being a prisoner or being on the run. I want my freedom. I want to live my life the way I want to, not how someone else pictures it. My way."

"And you can only do that alone?" Travis pointed to her glass but she shook her head. She didn't need more alcohol; her mind was already swimming. He rose and poured himself another finger of whiskey.

"I don't know," she answered honestly. "That's something I'm not thinking about right now. Until Alan is out of my life permanently I'm not making a whole lot of future plans."

"Fair enough." Travis drained his glass and slapped it down on the table. "How about I show you your room? You've got to be exhausted. I'm not sure when West will get here and it could be quite awhile. No sense in you waiting up."

He didn't say anything about getting any sleep for himself she noticed. When he'd ushered her into his beautiful home he'd set a fancy computerized alarm system after locking the door. She'd also glimpsed the shoulder holster he kept tucked under his dark blue suit. Her security was being taken seriously and for that she was relieved and grateful.

But she hated that he and West had to do it. She'd brought trouble into the lives of people she cared about even if she hadn't planned to. If she'd left a month ago as she should have none of this would have happened.

"Thank you. And thank you for coming with us on the trip. I'm sure you have a lot more important things to be doing other than babysitting me."

"I'm looking forward to the trip, actually. Besides, with West suspending his campaign to take you to Vegas I've got a lot of free time on my hands."

Gigi didn't believe him for a second. He ran all of the Anderson family holdings and there probably weren't enough hours in the day to do it, but it was nice of him to pretend otherwise.

"I feel badly about that. I know how everyone feels about Cavendish and if he wins because West can't campaign…"

She let her voice trail away but Travis was already shaking his head. "I don't think you could talk West out of this no matter what. Your life or his candidacy? Honey, it's not even a contest."

Not sure what she'd done to deserve West's devotion, she stood and followed Travis up the stairs, the carpet so thick and lush her shoes seemed to sink into the floor. Her room was at the end of the hall all decorated in shades of blue and gold.

"It's lovely," she exclaimed. "You have excellent taste. Your home is like something out of a magazine."

"Thank you. It's missing something though. I'm just not sure what. Maybe a movie screening room or a wood shop will be next."

Gigi couldn't imagine this house needing anything extra but if he did then she'd keep her mouth shut. What did she know about homes after all? She'd never really had one.

"Good night, Travis."

"Good night, Gigi."

Travis closed the door softly behind him and she barely made it to the bed before her knees crumpled underneath her. She leaned back against the headboard, the events of the evening playing over and over in her head and making her want to scream with frustration.

She was tired of this. All of it. Tired of being a victim. Tired of crying. Tired of playing hide and seek with a madman.

She wanted her life back.

West had held out the first hope she'd felt in years and she wouldn't waste it. With his help she'd shake off the past and start building a new, better future.

Only one question remained. Would it be with him? Or without him?

Chapter Twelve

IS GIGI ASLEEP?" West asked when he entered Travis's house just after three in the morning. Exhausted and irritable, he wanted a stiff whiskey and a decent night's sleep. In that order.

"She went up about twelve-thirty."

Travis was playing mind reader and poured West a drink without being asked. West accepted it gratefully and sank down into a leather chair with a sigh of relief. It had been one long damn night and things weren't going to get much better in the coming days.

"I talked to her for a little bit and your girl has been through the wringer. A lot of people would have just folded their tent and given up. She's got backbone."

West knocked back the whiskey, enjoying the fire it created in his belly. It was exactly what he needed after the day he'd had.

"She'd gone through way too much for someone so young. We need to put this Morton guy out of business for good. Did Jason call with any more information from his government buddies?"

"No, but he did say he was planning on stopping by tomorrow." Travis glanced at the clock on the wall. "Make that today.

We need to update our plans based on this new information. Morton knows where she is. Now what was once a straightforward road trip has turned into a game of hide and seek."

A game West intended to win. Travis had texted him a copy of the picture that had in all probability tipped Morton off as to Gigi's whereabouts. They wouldn't make a mistake like that again. But of course West hadn't known that she was on the run at the time, but he did now and every precaution would be taken to ensure her safety.

"I'm working on getting us reinforcements for the trip to Vegas," West assured his brother. "Highly trained and armed to the teeth. He'll have to go through a fucking arsenal to get to her."

"If he can't get to her right away he might settle for you. Have you thought about that? The photo of you two was fairly damning. You're both looking at each other like you'd rather be in bed. That won't make the asshole too damn happy."

West snorted and poured himself another drink. "I can only hope he comes after me. I'd like to get this guy one on one. But I doubt he'll differentiate between me and anyone who is trying to keep her safe. He'll go after you or Jason just as quick. Are you ready for that?"

Travis's smile widened. "Damn straight I'm ready. Like you I wouldn't mind getting my clothes dirty and beating on this jerk for awhile. We might get a chance. We know he can be sloppy."

"Sloppy? What do you mean by that?"

"He sent a couple of his men to break into the house of the head of detectives. Shit, that was stupid. The article didn't mention your profession and he obviously didn't do much research into who the hell you are. Otherwise he would have waited until Gigi was alone."

West twirled the amber liquid in the bottom of the glass. "I checked Gigi's apartment myself before I came here. Somebody had broken in. Looking for her obviously. When she wasn't there they came for her at my place. Maybe they were desperate and afraid to call their boss and tell him they'd lost her."

"Desperate men make bad decisions. They're the most dangerous kind. I doubt Morton will make two mistakes in a row. If he has half a brain he'll do some digging into your background, and by extension into the entire Anderson family. I also have to wonder if he knows about Gigi's brother and sister. She was looking for them when she was with him. We could be walking into a trap."

"I haven't done anything dangerous in weeks," West laughed. "You're not getting scared are you?"

"No way. I'm looking forward to this as much as you are. Sitting behind a desk day in and day out gets old real fast."

Travis was an adrenaline junkie. Jumping out of airplanes. Bungee jumping off of bridges. Riding motorcycles hell for leather and messing up his leg in the process. He always said the best feeling in the world was fear mixed with excitement and your heart racing so fast a person can't count the beats.

In other words, Travis was a crazy bastard with a death wish.

"If Morton does do his homework on me it's only going to make him amp up the artillery. Trap or no trap, this whole damn situation just got more dangerous. For everyone."

✦   ✦   ✦

Alan Morton slammed down the phone into its cradle, his body shaking with rage. Punching his oak desk with a curled up fist, he beckoned to his right hand man Elliot.

"Tony and Frank fucked up. Frank's in the hospital and Tony's lying low. Apparently whoever Georgette's shacked up with met them with a gun. I need everything you can find on a West Anderson of Tremont, Montana." When Elliot hesitated Alan stood up and leaned forward to punctuate the urgency. "Now. And send in Joe on your way out."

"Will do."

The younger man practically ran out of Alan's office, his lips trembling in fear. Alan loved that part of being who he was. He loved the control he had over people's lives and playing with them was part and parcel of the game.

His favorite trick was to be sweet and nice to someone until they were lulled into a false sense of security, thinking he was harmless. Then...

Bam.

He showed them who they were fucking with. Elliot had learned quickly but every now and then he needed to be reminded who held the power.

"You wanted me, boss?"

Joe Stickler ambled into Alan's office but didn't take a seat without an invitation.

Good boy.

Alan had trained his second in command well.

"Tony and Frank botched the whole thing in Montana. I still don't have Georgette back where she belongs and that doesn't make me happy. I want you to run this personally. I have

Elliot looking into her boyfriend's background so maybe we'll find something there we can use. The article said his family was filthy rich and he was a spoiled playboy."

It had been pure luck that Joe had seen Georgette's photo on the news website. Alan had been looking for her for two goddamn years without much luck. She'd pay for putting him through this. Once he had her under his control again she'd be lucky to see the light of day for a decade. She needed him to keep her safe. It was that plain and simple.

Poor and struggling when he'd met her, he'd turned her into a lady with elegance and class. Someone he could dress up and show off. But she'd never been happy and had fought at every turn her prescribed role in this life. She wanted to have ideas and opinions. Just like Anna.

Georgette wanted freedom. A highly overrated state of which he would cure her of. Real freedom was a lie and an illusion. Everyone answered to someone in this world.

Georgette answered to Alan.

Alan answered to Caleb Deardon. As long as he kept Caleb happy Alan would stay rich…and alive.

"Why don't we just use—"

"No." Alan cut off Joe, knowing what he was about to suggest. "We're not that desperate yet. I'm keeping that in my pocket just in case. So Georgette has a boyfriend now? Don't make this into a big deal. We take him out and get her back. This isn't fucking rocket science. Just make it happen."

"Got it." Joe turned on his heel. "I'll report back when I have something."

Joe disappeared and Alan dug into the bottom of a desk

drawer, pulling out a manila folder. He spread the contents in front of him before picking up a snapshot of Georgette taken a few weeks before she'd left him. Dressed in a long white gown with her blonde hair piled artfully on top of her head and diamonds around her neck and wrist, she might have been mistaken for a princess or perhaps a movie star. She was that beautiful. Unsmiling in the photo, she was looking off into the distance completely unaware he'd been watching.

He hadn't thought much of it at the time but now he knew she'd been dreaming of something other than a life spent with him. At his side.

She needed him to take care of her, to love and protect her. She simply didn't understand how dangerous the world could be and that he would make sure she was safe.

It was time to bring her home.

Chapter Thirteen

G IGI'S EYES FLUTTERED open and then closed again, the sun pouring through the bedroom window. She could have sworn the drapes were closed last night but now they were wide open and clearly showing her she'd slept in quite late.

"Finally awake, sleepy head."

She cautiously opened one eye to see West striding out of the ensuite bathroom with nothing but a towel wrapped around his waist. How did he manage to look so damn good this early in the morning? A few rivulets of water ran down his muscular chest and she had to quell the urge to run her tongue over his washboard abs and lick away the moisture.

"What time is it?"

With a big yawn, Gigi sat up and rubbed at her eyes. The pillow next to her own was dented so it looked like West had joined her in bed at some point last night but she'd completely slept through it.

If it had been Alan she'd either be dead or on her way to Chicago tied up in the trunk of his car.

"A few minutes after nine. Throw on some clothes and we'll go down for breakfast. Travis is a really good cook. He'll make you his famous ham and cheese omelet."

Her stomach gurgled optimistically at the mention of food. She was starving.

"What time did you get in?"

"About three."

He had a strange expression on his face, kind of closed off as if he didn't want her reading his emotions. Normally he was completely open, so it looked like whatever news he had wasn't good.

"Just tell me. I can take it," Gigi sighed. He might as well just hit her with it. She'd survived worse and things were definitely not looking up after last night.

West scratched his chin and then sat down next to her on the bed. "Someone broke into your apartment last night. I'm guessing they went there first and when they couldn't find you they ended up at my place."

That made sense and wasn't surprising.

"And?" she prompted. "Is that all?"

West lifted up her hand and pressed a kiss to the knuckles. "The suspect that was hit last night? He's in a coma after surgery and can't tell us anything. The other guy is still at large."

The news kept getting better and better.

"So...what does that mean for me? Do you want to lock me up here until you catch the other guy?"

West frowned but then his expression quickly cleared. "I see what you're asking. The answer is no. We're not going to stay here like ducks in a shooting gallery waiting for someone to try and kill me and kidnap you. We're going to head to Vegas with a caravan of heavily armed and well-trained guards. I promised you'd see your brother and I intend to keep that promise. I know you've waited a long time for that to happen. It would be easy to say 'tough' since it's been years so you can wait a little longer, but that's just a crappy thing to do in my opinion. Especially how Morton kept you virtually a prisoner. I can't do the same thing and look myself in the mirror."

He was a man of his word, she'd always known that. But hearing that she was indeed going to see her brother soon made her heart squeeze tightly in her chest.

"Thank you. I know it only makes your job harder."

West shrugged and pulled her into his strong arms, the scent of his freshly scrubbed skin sending tingles of awareness through her limbs. She'd never intended to get this involved with West Anderson but here she was depending on him for her continued survival. It made her breathe easier but it also made her feel guilty as hell. He hadn't signed up for this knowingly.

"It would be easy to lock you up for weeks or months on end and tell you it's for your own good. I'm sure that wouldn't endear me to you though. My mission is clear, babe. Find your siblings and put Alan Morton behind bars. Sure, I could do the latter before the former but it would be cruel to make you wait that long. Let's reunite you with your brother and then get Morton."

"And then find Aubrey," she added softly, her heart squeezing in her chest remembering the last time she'd seen her sister. All curls and big brown eyes, Aubrey had been so young and innocent. "I can't believe I might have my family back soon. It seems so unreal. You know, to have hope again. It's been so long."

His rough fingers traced her jaw and her breath caught in her chest. "I want to give that back to you. I want you to have the life you deserve."

A life with him?

The unspoken question hung there between them as she gazed into his green eyes. If she came out of this alive – and he managed to put Alan behind bars – she'd finally be free. Free enough to contemplate having a real future. Unfortunately at the moment she couldn't predict much past her next meal. By the time all this ugliness was over he might not want her anymore.

Instead of answering him she leaned in and brushed her lips against his firm, warm mouth. She didn't have the words to express feelings she barely understood. He was the most important person in her life and her attempt at leaving him had been like ripping off her own limbs.

Was that love? She had no idea. He was a man worth loving, of that she was certain. But the thought of putting herself out there…making herself vulnerable again…was terrifying.

West didn't seem to mind her non-verbal reply. With no hesitation he quickly took control of the kiss until she found herself pressed into the mattress under his delicious weight. Her fingers dug into his biceps as he nipped a trail down the sensitive cord of her neck, pushing aside the t-shirt she'd worn to bed to expose a bare shoulder.

She shuddered, heat sweeping through her body, scorching the flesh he was kissing and licking. His hands slid under her shirt, whisking it up and over her head before tossing it away without a second glance. He ran his tongue down to the curve of her breast and she tangled her fingers in his short dark hair. She could feel his smile against her skin as he nuzzled an already hard nipple before lapping at the tip. Moving restlessly, her lids fluttered closed and a moan escaped from her lips when his teeth scraped the sensitive bud.

"Yes," she hissed, pleasure bubbled and fizzed through her veins. His fingers slid down her torso, over her ribcage and belly, to stroke the sensitive flesh of her inner thighs. A groan escaped her lips and she lifted her hips in anticipation of the ecstasy she knew his touch would bring.

West gave a knowing chuckle, his breath a warm breeze across the tips of her breasts. sending a frisson of lightning straight to her toes. "Easy, babe. I'll give you what you need."

She barely heard him over the roar in her ears but she didn't doubt him for a moment. Since the day they'd met West Anderson had seemed to know her deepest, darkest needs and how to fulfill them. He stoked a fire inside that couldn't be quenched by anyone or anything else.

He was one of a kind. And for now he belonged to her.

She wouldn't think about tomorrow or the next day. These last few years she'd survived by concentrating on the present. It had been the thing that had kept her sane. But could it save her immeasurable heartbreak? That might be asking too much.

His callused thumb glided over her clit, already swollen and sensitive, and her body bucked in response to his feather-light touch. She scrunched the sheets in her tight fists when he slid a thick digit into her slick channel, her muscles hugging him tightly as a coil of arousal clenched in her abdomen.

Slowly, as if he had all the time in the world, he grazed his thumb back and forth over her clit while rubbing a sensitive spot deep inside, keeping her teetering on the edge but never enough to send her over.

Her breath came in pants and the world seemed to melt away as he whispered hot, filthy words in her ear. She bit her lip to keep pleas of mercy from falling from her lips but West would have none of that. In that dark, deep voice that could do all manner of naughty things to her libido, he exhorted her to tell him exactly what she wanted. Needed. Desired.

"Fuck me," she whispered, her voice tortured and breathless. "Fuck me hard and fast. I need it. I need you. Make me come. Now."

It was always like this. The heat. The urgency. The over-whelming need to get *closer* to him. It was at moments like this she forgot everything. The past no longer mattered and the fear dissolved away. It was Gigi and West and everything they could make each other feel. Nothing else.

West ripped away the towel, his hard cock slapping against his ridged abdomen. She reached out and wrapped her fingers around him, sliding them up and down his impressive length. He groaned and stilled her movements even as one hand reached for his pants flung on a chair, rummaging for a condom. Pulling out the square, he pressed a kiss to her belly and then her hipbone.

He rolled on the condom and then lined himself up with her entrance. She slid her legs farther apart and grabbed his hips to guide him, her nails digging into the flesh and leaving crescent marks in their wake.

With one deft stroke he sheathed himself balls deep, a shudder running through his muscular frame as he held himself still, his face a mask of concentration.

"So damn tight," he growled. "So fucking good."

Gigi was beyond speech. The sensation of feeling so delightfully full was heaven on earth. She swayed her hips as West slowly began to thrust, easy at first but building speed quickly until he was riding her hard and fast.

She loved every minute of it.

Every stroke sent her higher until she was floating among stars that glittered and popped. Their bodies shimmered with sweat and she wrapped her legs around his waist urging him on.

Her orgasm took her by surprise with its intensity. Like a tidal wave, it stole her breath and took control of her body turning her world topsy-turvy. She watched as West achieved his own climax, his eyes closed and his head thrown back, teeth bared in a snarl of sublime male satisfaction.

"Holy hell, woman. You pack a wallop," he laughed shakily, rolling to his back and tucking her into his side.

Gigi's heart rate began to slow and she lazily traced circles on his chest, in no hurry to start the day. Whatever was out there wasn't as good as what they had here. If only they could stay in bed forever it would be perfect.

Assuming anything could be perfect in the first place.

Eventually West levered up and gave her a devilish grin. "I need to take another shower. How about you join me so we can save some water?"

Paradise might not last but she could extend it a little. "That's an offer I can't refuse. Maybe you could wash my back?"

"And a few other things, babe." His exaggerated leer made her giggle and she watched his very fine ass stride across the room. "I'll get the water warm but don't make me wait too long."

Determined not to dwell on what lay ahead of them, Gigi threw back the covers. "I'm right behind you, handsome."

She'd follow him anywhere.

Chapter Fourteen

"IF YOU NEED to go to the bathroom now is the time to do it."

West brought the SUV to a halt next to the gas pump. It was just past midnight and they'd been on the road since sundown. They'd only seen a few cars on the lonesome stretch of highway which made for a long, boring but stress-free drive.

They'd brought with them every man West could muster. Jason in his pickup truck led the parade with his friend Jared Monroe riding shotgun while Travis brought up the rear in his mint condition cherry red 1967 Mustang convertible that he'd spent thousands of hours and dollars restoring. In the passenger seat was an Anderson family cousin, Shane, who had agreed to help out. He worked with Travis running the oil drilling division and shared West's brother's passion for adrenaline rushes. A little wild but down to earth, he was a good addition to the team. Logan Wright couldn't make it due to family illness but he might join them later.

"I do. I'll get us some snacks too while I'm in there."

Gigi started to push open the door but West reached across her body and stayed her movements. She wasn't going anywhere alone. Jared and Shane would accompany her and keep an eye out for any trouble. So far it had been an uneventful trip and West hoped to hell it would stay that way.

"They're going to do a sweep of the inside. The emptier it is the better. Be patient."

With a long-suffering sigh Gigi's hand fell away from the door handle. "You have a lot of nerve telling me to be patient, Westin Anderson."

That was one hundred percent true. She'd waited years to find her family, not to mention being on the run to avoid Alan Morton. She was the personification of patience.

"Point taken. But I still need you to wait for a minute."

The walls of the convenience store were mostly glass and West could see Jared and Shane walking up and down the aisles, their gazes sweeping over the entire location. Jason and Travis stayed back with the vehicles in case they needed to make a swift exit. Jared stepped out of the building and jogged over to the SUV.

"All clear. Just the two clerks."

"Did you check the ladies' room?"

Jared nodded, his body tense and alert. "Shane did. It's empty. We'll guard the door while she's in there."

"Okay, babe. Let's see how quick this stop can be, okay? We need to get back on the road."

West had estimated the trip, if they drove all night and included stops for food and gas, at about fifteen hours give or take thirty minutes or so. That would put them in Vegas about noon and in desperate need of sleep.

Gigi hiked her purse over her shoulder and allowed Jared to

hustle her into the store. Still keeping an eye out, West swung out of the driver's seat and popped open the gas cap. He loved this truck but damn, it ate fuel. Stopping so often was definitely going to slow them down although he still probably got better mileage than Travis's muscle car.

While West refilled the tank another car pulled in to the pumps, a late model sedan. Four doors. Dark tinted windows. Very dark. He didn't see windows tinted that dark too often on a conservative family vehicle. It had been West's experience that the only people who had windows that dark were those with something to hide. It also seemed strange that another car was in the middle of nowhere at an almost deserted gas station when West hadn't seen another vehicle in almost thirty minutes.

Suspicion put him immediately on edge, his blood pumping in his veins. Pulling the brim of his hat down over his face, he finished pumping fuel and pocketed the receipt, keeping his gaze focused on the vehicle. A man – maybe late twenties or early thirties – hopped out of the driver's side and began filling his tank.

West searched the man's silhouette for a gun of some sort but nothing looked out of the ordinary. The driver's white button down shirt was tucked into a pair of blue jeans and there was no place to hide a weapon unless he had it tucked into his boot, which was a possibility. Or maybe a knife. Or perhaps it was a guy who was simply getting gas and not dangerous at all. West scanned the vehicle but the windows were too dark to be able to tell if there was a companion of any sort. If there was one he or she didn't appear to be planning to get out of the car.

The brake lights of another vehicle driving by on the service road came on and the car slowed down almost to a crawl. Instead of pulling into the station it inched down the road and then unexpectedly veered into an empty lot with an old boarded up fast food joint before cutting the headlights. No one exited the vehicle but the engine continued to idle.

Strange behavior but not necessarily dangerous. It could be someone checking directions on their phone or even just making a call. He needed to remind himself that criminals weren't around every corner. His job could sometimes bend his world view in a biased direction.

His gaze slid back to the suspicious sedan but the driver was simply standing there filling the tank and whistling an old Guns and Roses song. Glancing over his shoulder, West could see Gigi and Shane out of the corner of his eye paying at the counter and then heading for the car. Their arms were full of drinks and snacks but Jared stopped them at the door, checking the parking lot before letting them out.

Jason heaved a sigh of relief when he saw her coming towards him, looking more beautiful than anyone should have a right to after being cooped up in a car for several hours in the middle of the night. She'd left her golden blonde hair loose today and it bounced around her shoulders, tempting him to reach out and run his fingers through the silky strands.

"I loaded up on junk food," she said with a smile. "We'll be wired from all the sugar."

"I'm going to need a detox diet when we get back home," laughed Shane, heading for his vehicle. "But I'm going to enjoy it for now."

In contrast to Shane's ebullient mood Jared was his usual

quiet and controlled self, barely smiling and constantly on alert. The man could relax and have fun with the best of them but he took his job damn seriously.

West walked around the truck and opened the door of the SUV for Gigi, using his own body as a shield in front while Jared had her back. He thought they were in the clear when the passenger door of the dark windowed sedan swung open and the fluorescent overhead lights glinted off the metal of a gun barrel.

"Down!"

Adrenaline surged through West and he shoved Gigi to the hard concrete, his body covering hers. Jared had pulled his own piece from his shoulder holster as the sound of gunfire assailed West's eardrums but he could barely hear it over the thundering of his own heart.

In his peripheral vision he could see Travis coming up behind the sedan driver – who had acquired a firearm at some point – and knocking him to the ground with a rifle butt to the back of the head. He didn't have a chance to get to the passenger or the two men who had jumped from the back seat though as a spray of bullets was directed his way, driving him back to his own vehicle where Shane was stationed near the trunk.

West could feel the quaking of Gigi's body as she lay underneath him, pressed into the unforgiving concrete. If he could get her out of this alive she'd probably have some nasty bruises from him slamming her into the ground.

"Hang in there, babe. I'm going to get you to safety," he whispered in her ear. She didn't answer but the whimpering ceased although her lips still trembled with fear.

Get her in the car. Get her to safety.

"Can you handle this?" West hissed to Jared who was using the door of the SUV as a shield. The back window shattered as a bullet ran through it, throwing glass in every direction. "I need to get Gigi out of here."

"Go," Jared growled. "We got this. We'll meet up with you later."

With one man down now the gunfire paused and West didn't hesitate for a moment. Grunting with the effort, he pushed to his knees and lifted Gigi with him, practically stuffing her into the passenger side of the vehicle.

"Stay. Don't fucking move."

Gigi nodded, tears streaming down her face, her eyes wide with fear.

The pavement digging into his flesh, West crawled on his belly under the door and pulled his department issue firearm. With the driver of the sedan unconscious the three henchmen were outnumbered and outgunned. It was only a matter of time but they weren't going to give up easily. Right now they were alternating between hunkering down in the car and leaning out of the window, spraying bullets intermittently.

"I'll cover you." West lifted his gun and shot off a few rounds as Jared quickly crawled back to the lead vehicle. Jason had positioned himself in the bed of the truck and Jared jumped in with him before signaling with his arm that West should get the hell out of there.

West didn't need to be told twice. Swinging his body back under the door he slid over Gigi who was curled into a ball in the passenger seat. Smart girl that she was, she'd somehow managed to reach the ignition and start the SUV. He stayed low as he settled into the driver's side, gunning the engine and careening out of the gas station.

"Stay down," he commanded, glancing to make sure she obeyed him. He didn't need her head popping up, creating the perfect target for Morton's henchman.

All previous plans he'd made were blown to smithereens. West was flying by the seat of his pants and he needed to get Gigi out of the line of fire before he could think about the implications of what had happened back there. With his government and law contacts Jason would be able to handle whatever local law enforcement threw at him, although West would rather his friends get out of there before the cops showed up. He didn't relish the idea of being out on the road. Alone. No protection. No help. Completely exposed. It wasn't how he'd pictured this trip but it was now the reality.

If tonight was any indication Alan Morton was serious as a heart attack about getting Gigi back and killing West in the process. West mentally battled back and forth before finally choosing the main highway over a back road. The cops in this area would know the ins and outs of routes off the beaten path better than West would and he didn't want to get trapped in an unfamiliar area with no exits. The highway offered more options and kept them moving at a high speed but toward what he hadn't decided.

Did Morton's men follow them and wait for an ambush opportunity? Or did they know Gigi was heading for Vegas specifically? It might be a good idea to go in another direction for a little while and see what transpired. It might not be a bad idea to change vehicles either. This one was full of bullet holes and a broken back window. It screamed *Gun Fight at the OK Corral* to anyone who saw it.

"Are we safe?" Gigi asked, her voice shaky. She was stilled curled up in the passenger seat, broken glass in her hair and on her shoulders.

West rubbed the back of his neck, his skin slick with sweat. "It depends on how you define safe, babe. We're out of the line of fire. For the moment. But I need to figure out what to do now. Do you think Morton knows about your brother in Las Vegas?"

"I don't know. He might. I talked about Zach and Aubrey a lot. He knew I was looking for them."

Gigi began to sit up but he put his hand on her shoulder and pressed her back into the seat.

"I need you to stay down for now. I have to figure out what we're going to do."

She looked as if she was going to object for a moment but then acquiesced and sunk back down below window level.

"I'm scared."

Those two simple words tore at West's heart and he reached over to stroke the soft skin of her arm. The lights on the highway flew by as he pressed heavily on the accelerator, putting more miles between them and Morton's men.

"I'm not going to let anything happen to you. Trust me."

"I trust you with my life, West."

Her life. But not her love. She'd been holding a part of herself back since the day he'd met her.

"Everything is going to be okay. Just stay down while I put some distance between us and that gas station."

A million questions whirled in and out of his overloaded brain, making his temples ache and his stomach churn with acid. The station probably had security cameras which would mean law enforcement would have at the very least a description of his vehicle, or even worse, his license plate number. He couldn't keep Gigi safe if he was locked away in some small town county jail even if it was only for a short time. He had to keep moving.

West glimpsed an old ramshackle red barn on the side of the road. They sped past it but not before it sparked a memory of long ago. Would his friend still be there? His family had lived on that land for the last hundred years so the odds were good.

West knew exactly where he was headed. If anyone could help him it was Wyatt Stone.

Chapter Fifteen

CRAMPED AND SCARED Gigi shifted in her seat, laying her head on the console between herself and West, her face pressed to the cool leather. He'd tried to reassure and comfort her, explaining that they were going to find an old Army buddy of his that lived near here but he still wouldn't let her sit up in the seat. By the stiffness in his shoulders and his tight jaw it was clear he was angry and frustrated. A perfectionist, he didn't like surprises and he hated losing control of a situation even more. Her alpha male liked to give the orders and he expected them to be obeyed without question.

The truck bumped and rolled, tossing her around enough that she had to grab on to the door handle. The lights from the highway were long gone and she could see nothing from her vantage point but an inky black sky speckled with a star here and there. The forecast called for rain which made getting a new back window even more important.

She shouldn't have been shocked that Alan sent his minions after her and West. Now that he'd found out about where she was living she'd known he'd be determined to bring her back. He was obsessed with controlling her. Making her obey. He was sick and he didn't care who he hurt. West. His brothers or friends.

If he managed to find her and bring her back to him? She had no doubt he'd punish her. Something painful that she'd never forget. She's seen his inhuman cruelty only on a few occasions but those incidents had been branded on her consciousness as if they happened yesterday.

The SUV turned onto a rutted road that almost jolted her teeth loose. It was a relief when he brought the truck to a halt and put the vehicle in park.

"Wait here."

West patted her shoulder before exiting the SUV, locking the door behind him. She heard his boots on wooden stair steps and then a banging on what was probably a front door. A dog began to bark and growl and then soft voices spoke but she couldn't make out the actual words. West's footsteps came closer and she lifted her head slightly to try and see their location.

Knocking softly on the passenger window, West beckoned to Gigi. "It's okay. Come on out."

Gigi pushed the car door open and let West help her uncurl her body, cramped and hurting from crouching for so long. His strong fingers rubbed her shoulders as she followed him back up the porch steps to where a tall, muscular man with dark hair stood in the doorway partially outlined by the lamplight. Dressed in blue jeans and a half unbuttoned red flannel shirt, she placed his age at about forty due to a few silver strands at his temples.

"Come on in and get comfortable, Miss. Are you hungry or thirsty?"

The man's voice rumbled in the quiet but it was a warm and friendly sound that drew her toward him. She stepped across the threshold and into the old fashioned log home that was small but neat and tidy. A yellow lab with a wagging tail hovered close by, too well trained to jump on her but obviously excited about a visitor that might scratch his belly.

"I'll pull the truck into the barn." West gave her a quick hug and dropped a kiss on her forehead. "Let Wyatt take care of you. He's a good friend and I'd trust him with my life. Hell, I'd trust him with *your* life. I'm going to hide our vehicle just in case anyone comes snooping around. Give me five minutes."

She wouldn't have objected to his leaving her alone with this other man but she felt slightly bereft as he jogged down the steps and into the night. Wyatt closed the door behind her and pointed down a hallway, giving her a sympathetic smile.

"There's a bathroom down there if you want to get freshened up."

Now that sounded like heaven. She felt grimy and sweaty, which really wasn't all that bad considering she'd been caught in a gunfire fight not long ago. It was only delayed shock that kept her from falling apart completely. She was holding onto her sanity by her fingernails but losing her grip rapidly. She hadn't wanted to fall apart in front of West when he was trying so hard to take care of her and keep her safe. But now that she was inside this warm and cozy house the numbness was beginning to wear off and horror was taking its place. What she really needed was a big shot of whiskey and for West to hold her for the next several hours to keep the nightmares at bay.

Once locked behind the bathroom door she splashed cold

water on her face, staring into the small mirror over the sink. Her skin was pale and her eyes red-rimmed from crying. She looked a mess and felt worse. The whole trip which had begun with such promise had gone to shit.

Alan would never leave her alone.

Mentally she gave herself a pointed, tough pep talk. There was no time to feel sorry for herself. She was ass deep in a mess and hopefully with West's help she'd claw her way out. She hadn't fooled herself that it would be easy. Or pretty. The fact was this was probably going to get uglier and messier before it was over.

She quickly ran a comb through her hair and rejoined Wyatt, who was now in the kitchen heating up a kettle. True to his word West was back in the house shrugging off his jacket but leaving on his shoulder holster.

"Gigi, have you had a chance to meet my old friend Wyatt Stone?"

"We haven't yet been formally introduced." Gigi held out her hand to the handsome man who had graciously taken them in. "I'm Gigi. It's nice to meet you."

"Wyatt." Her hand seemed to disappear in his large one but despite his size he seemed cognizant of his strength. "It's nice to meet you too. Are you hungry or thirsty?"

West slapped his friend on the back. "I don't know about Gigi but I could use a drink, my friend. A strong one."

"I've got some whiskey in the cabinet. I also have some chicken casserole I can warm up in the oven if you like." Wyatt reached up over the stove and pulled down a bottle and three glasses. "Are you going to tell me what's going on or is it classified?"

"How much time do you got?"

Wyatt looked around the house, clearly empty except for himself and the dog. "I need to feed the chickens around sun up. Besides that I've got nothing pressing."

West lowered himself into a kitchen chair and indicated that Gigi should do the same. "I can tell you but you might not believe me."

Chuckling, Wyatt poured out three fingers of whiskey. "Those are the best kinds of stories from my experience. What have you got yourself into now?"

Danger. Gigi had dragged West into a pile of it and she didn't know how to get him – and herself – out of it.

They couldn't go back. They couldn't stay here.

The only way to move was forward.

✦ ✦ ✦

"SOMETHING IS WRONG. Something more than just the situation we're in."

Gigi pulled the covers over her suddenly chilled body. They were tucked up in Wyatt's spare bedroom after having a bite of dinner and a stiff drink. West had told the entire story sparing few details, but somehow managing not to make her sound like an idiot. She was grateful for his thoughtfulness but with everything that had happened she didn't deserve his protection. It was all her fault they were ass deep in alligators.

While she'd soaked in a hot bath West and Wyatt had stayed huddled in the kitchen, their voices unintelligible from where she was but the deeply serious tone unmistakable. With West's brothers and friends God knows where, they were on their own. It was a terror filled thought that had tears running down her face as she'd struggled to control her overwhelming emotions.

Sitting all alone in that tub, she'd allowed the horrors of the evening to finally sink in.

But she hadn't come this far to fall apart now when she was so close to finding her family. She'd wiped away the tears and pulled herself together. She was a fighter and had been all her life. Nothing had ever been easy or peaceful.

West slipped between the sheets, his expression grim and pale. "I finally was able to talk to Jason. It was a fucking mess there after we left. They managed to take out two men of the four plus shoot out two tires on the sedan. When the remaining men realized they weren't going to win they abandoned their friends and hightailed it out of there."

"The police? Did they get there?"

Lips flattening into a thin line, West shrugged. "Probably. I'm sure one of the station clerks called 911. The guys didn't hang around to find out. They headed for the nearest hospital."

Gigi's fingers clutched the soft blanket and her stomach twisted into tight knots. "Hospital? Was someone hurt?"

"Shane got a slug right in the gut. They were terrified he would bleed out. They got on the road right away but Jason called an old buddy from the government and I guess they sent out one of those helicopter ambulances. So now Shane is in a hospital in Salt Lake City having emergency surgery. In the meantime Jason is answering a lot of questions from the authorities. They're not going to get to leave any time soon from what he said. As a general rule law enforcement is very interested in shoot outs with non-locals."

Gigi had to concentrate on her breathing as the room seemed to blur and spin. If Shane died she would never forgive herself. She didn't expect West to forgive her either.

"Is Shane going to be okay?"

West fell back against the cushions, a muscle working in his jaw. "Jason said the doctors were optimistic but they won't know if the surgery is successful for another few hours. I told Jason to call me as soon as Shane is in recovery."

Gigi buried her head in her hands, guilt swamping any feelings of fear she'd harbored earlier. "I'm so sorry. So very sorry. You should go to your cousin. Be there for him."

"Are you kidding? I won't leave you. Jason and Travis are with him and as they reminded me there's nothing I can do for Shane right now except pray."

"All of this is my fault."

"No." West's tone was stern but his arms were gentle as he pulled her close to pillow her cheek on his chest. "This is all Morton's fault. I won't leave you when we're so close to ending all of this once and for all. Shane's a tough son of a bitch and I believe he'll be fine. His mother is on her way to the hospital to be with him. He'll be surrounded by people who love him. He knows that my job is to protect you."

Gigi let out a long sigh as West played with an errant strand of hair, tickling her chin. "Your job should be running for mayor. You're missing the last debate and we may not even get back in time for you to vote for yourself. What if Cavendish wins again?"

"If he wins then we start a petition for a recall," West replied.

"I never really wanted to be mayor in the first place but I didn't want Cavendish to win another four years. The bastard's ruining Tremont. Everyone in town knows who I am and what I stand for. They don't need to hear me speak at a debate to understand what I believe in. If they want me as mayor they'll vote for me...whether I'm there or not. If I lose, I lose."

"I think you're more competitive than that." Gigi traced circles on West's bare chest. "I think you kind of want to win."

"You sound like Travis. He thinks everyone is as cutthroat as he is. I'm really okay if I lose. I just wish Cavendish wouldn't be the winner, that's all."

"He is sort of a jerk."

Mayor Cavendish came into the diner at least once a week and expected everyone to make a fuss over him like he was royalty. Gigi couldn't understand that sense of entitlement.

"He's a major league asshole," West retorted with a laugh. "But that doesn't mean he doesn't have a few friends. Time will tell how this will all work out. But hear me loud and clear, babe. I'm not going anywhere. I'll be with you every step of the way until Morton is behind bars. You can't get rid of me that easily, you know."

Gigi shouldn't feel relieved at his definitive statement but her breathing immediately became easier with his assurances.

"What are we going to do now? Do you have a plan?"

"I'm putting one together. I've talked to Jason and to Wyatt as well. I think we both need a few hours of sleep before we make any final decisions. Are you worried? I won't let anything happen to you."

He'd been saying that over and over since he'd found out

about Alan and now that she'd seen him in action she was starting to really believe it. No matter what happened he would stand by her.

It was a frightening and humbling action on his part.

She'd spent so much time keeping him at arm's length, pushing him away with both hands. He easily could have turned and left when she needed him the most.

"I trust you completely," she assured him, knowing in her heart it was the truth. "I was just wondering what we do now that we don't have anyone to make the trip with us."

"We'll be okay. I have a trick or two up my sleeve. In the meantime let's get some sleep. Everything will look better in the morning."

Gigi glanced at the bedside clock. "Morning is only a few hours away, handsome."

"Then everything will look better midday. Now close your eyes."

Gigi obeyed but not for long. She was too wired to fall asleep easily although West must have been exhausted. His chest was rising and falling gently, soft snores in an even rhythm. Cuddling close she relived the gun battle at the gas station over and over, knowing without a doubt that she would be on her way to Chicago if West hadn't been there.

She absolutely trusted him with her life. Could she trust him with her heart?

Chapter Sixteen

"G ODDAMIT." ALAN MORTON smashed his fist down on the desk, ignoring the shot of pain that ran up his arm. He was too fucking angry to pay it any attention. His men had screwed up. Again. "You could have killed her. What were they thinking, pulling their guns like that?"

Georgette had been in the middle of a firefight between the men he'd sent to collect her and her bodyguards. If she'd been killed or even injured he'd take great pleasure in beating the idiot who did it to death. Slowly. He'd want the man to know he was going to die…eventually. The asshole would be praying for death when Alan was done with him.

"She had five bodyguards, boss. There was no way they could have taken her without firing," the younger man stuttered, his face turning a distinct shade of reddish-purple. "I checked into that boyfriend of hers and he was Special Forces in the military. His brother worked for the DEA. They all knew how to handle a gun and one of them gave Steve a concussion and a broken arm."

Alan hated whining and excuses and this guy was full of both. Finding men who didn't lie down and give up when faced with a little adversity was almost impossible these days.

"Where is she now?"

He sat down behind his desk and rested his chin on his stee-pled fingers, breathing in and out slowly to try and regulate the rage churning inside of him. Every day that Georgette wasn't in this house and under his control was a day of her moving farther away from him. Once she was back it would take months to create the docile and obedient creature she had once been.

But of course this time he had something to help motivate her.

The man swallowed hard, his Adam's apple bobbing in his throat. "We don't know. One of the guards drove her away and our guys weren't able to follow because their tires had been shot out. We assume they're still headed for Las Vegas."

Alan slowly sat back in the leather chair, his hands tightening into fists. He would simply have to take care of this himself. He couldn't trust anyone with something this important. Georgette needed to come home.

He knew just what to do.

"We've had men stationed in Vegas for the last year," the man pointed out. "I'll tell them to get ready."

"Tell them to do nothing. They are to keep their distance. Follow and report only."

"I don't understand."

"I know." Alan inwardly chuckled at the young man's con-fused expression. With an IQ of 150 he was used to running intellectual circles around most of the people he met. Rarely did anyone challenge him. He liked it that way. "They won't be in Las Vegas for long. They're coming to Chicago. They're coming to us."

✦　✦　✦

"HOPEFULLY WYATT WON'T be long."

West handed Gigi a straw for her iced tea and she accepted it with shaking hands. They were sitting in a truck in the parking lot of the Mixed Martial Arts center where Zach worked as an instructor. Wyatt had agreed to not only lend them his Ford-350 extended cab but also accompanied them to Las Vegas, helping to keep Gigi safe.

It was good to see Wyatt getting out of his self-imposed exile. Since he'd left the service a few years before he'd practically hidden himself away on that lonely piece of property, only leaving when he absolutely needed something like food.

Wyatt had come back from the Middle East to nothing. His parents had passed away while he was deployed and his wife had left him for his best friend after admitting the child she carried wasn't his either. West's friend had moved back to his childhood home, adopted a dog, and retreated from the world. It was probably the fact that Gigi was also alone that made Wyatt want to help.

Luckily there had been no trouble during the drive down nor when they'd checked into the hotel. West doubted that Morton had given up, however. His cop instincts told him this was the lull before the storm.

Gigi of course was nervous about meeting her brother and so far all of West's assurances hadn't made anything better. She was practically vibrating in her seat with excitement and more than a little fear. West had stayed in the vehicle with her, sending

Wyatt in to find Zachary Rogers and talk to him. If they were still being followed – and West had no reason to doubt that – sending in an unfamiliar face might throw them off, at least temporarily.

"It's just so overwhelming really. I'm going to see Zach after all these years. I've missed him so much." Gigi's voice caught and her fingers flexed around the cup, the knuckles white. "I just hope…you know…that he wants to see me."

West frowned and shook his head. "Why on earth would he not want to see you? He's your brother. Didn't you say he took care of you and your sister when your mother couldn't?"

Her lips curved into a smile. "He made the best macaroni and cheese in the world. You know, the kind in a box. It was really good though. I don't know what he did to make it special but somehow it was. He made everything seem better. Even if it really sucked like when we couldn't go to the movies like our friends. He'd help us build a fort out of blankets and chairs or we'd play hide and seek in the house. It was the little things he did that made our lives okay. Honestly all I've ever wanted was to have a normal life and a normal family."

West had a sad suspicion that rabid hunger made Zach's mac and cheese delicious. From what Gigi had told him her mother had barely provided food and shelter for her three children. West made a silent promise to himself to personally thank Zachary Rogers for caring for Gigi and her sister when no one else would.

"It sounds like he's going to be thrilled to see you, babe. I bet he's missed you as much as you've missed him."

She plucked at her blue jeans, her gaze directed at the floor. "Maybe he feels he's better off without us. He missed so much having to take care of us. Maybe he's happier now."

Jesus, Mary, and Joseph. West's woman was so fucked up about love, family, and relationships. It wasn't her fault, of course. She'd had few if any role models and then when she'd thought she'd found someone who cared he turned out to be a batshit crazy criminal who would rather see her dead than free from his mad dictator-like control.

"Babe," West began, turning his body towards hers and lacing their fingers together. "If you love someone caring for them isn't a burden. It's a privilege. He might be happy but I doubt he's *happier* without you. You never stopped loving him and I bet he's never stopped loving you."

More staring at the floor, her shoulders stiff with tension. "I don't think our mother loved us very much. My foster family cared but they didn't love me or anything."

Where was she going with this?

"Your mother had an addiction problem so I doubt she was capable of deep emotions. As for your foster mom and dad it sounds like they cared very much but maybe it wasn't what you hoped for from a parental figure."

She lifted her head and looked him in the eye. "Maybe I'm just not all that lovable. Some people aren't, you know. I might be one of those people who are nice and everything but just don't inspire great love."

Gigi was completely serious. He'd obviously done a lousy job of showing her just how amazing and spectacular she was. How he'd fallen ass over tea kettle for her and hadn't been the same since.

"That's the biggest load of bull I've ever heard," he said

bluntly, watching her eyes widen with surprise. "Do you remember the day we first met? That day in the diner? You knocked me on my butt with your beautiful whiskey-colored eyes and your teasing smile. I was so hard I had to sit there and have two extra cups of coffee before I was in a decent enough state to leave. That's what you do to me."

"That's just sex."

"Is it?" he challenged. "Acting like a teenager with a crush isn't all that normal for me now that I'm a grown ass man. I followed you around like you were a rock star if you'll remember. It took forever to convince you to go out with me."

Gigi laughed and slapped him lightly on his shoulder. "Only Westin Anderson the biggest stud in Tremont would think a week was forever. Considering I never intended to go on a date – let alone sleep with you – that's pretty darn quick if you ask me. My acceptance was inevitable when you smiled at me and showed off that dimple in your cheek."

She was tracing that dimple with her finger now and his heart quickened in response. What she could do with a simple touch was positively dangerous.

"People love you, Gigi. My mom and dad think you're the best thing that's ever happened to me. My brothers and cousins adore you and everyone in Tremont thinks you're a total sweetheart. If you don't feel their love it's because you won't open yourself up to it. I get why you would protect yourself that way but we're going to put Morton behind bars. You'll get your life back. Somehow you are going to have to find a way to let people in. You're going to have to let me in."

His Gigi was a fighter but it was clear she'd rather be shot at than take a chance on opening her heart to love. And him.

"I'm not sure I know how. I don't think I can. Not after all this time."

She wasn't just talking about the last two years she'd been on the run. This was about her whole damn life and for a moment West felt despair take a hold of his gut. He didn't know how to turn around a lifetime of thinking she wasn't good enough.

He might have thought it was a lost cause but then he saw the light of hope in her eyes. She wanted to believe. To feel love. Give and receive. She was scared as hell but that didn't mean it was hopeless.

It was *hopeful*.

He'd need to go out on a limb if he wanted any sort of a chance. This was no time for any of his commitment phobia bullshit. He'd been dancing around his feelings all this time, protecting his own heart. He was supposed to the strong man in this relationship but he'd been just as weak and chicken shit.

Pathetic. It stopped at this moment.

"You'd better figure it out because I love you. And I've never said that to a woman before so that should tell you just how damn serious I am. You're lovable because I love you."

Her eyes went wide and her mouth fell open, clearly shocked at his declaration.

"I–I–"

She was speechless. *Good.* She needed to be knocked out of her complacency.

"I don't expect you to say it back. Not yet anyway. I get that you're scared and that you haven't really had any practice with this love stuff. So I'm okay with waiting. But I believe that you do love me so I'm going to be saying and showing it all the time. I don't mind not hearing the words but I do mind your emotions not being shown. Your actions mean more to me than mere words ever could."

"I–I...don't know what to say."

She didn't look scared or angry. If anything she didn't believe him. He'd have to spend some quality time showing her he was for real.

"You don't have to say anything. Just consider this me throwing down the gauntlet. I'm not giving up on you. I want us to be together so I'm going to become a major pain in your ass. When you need a push, I'll be there. Loving you, and just generally making it difficult to hide away."

His phone vibrated in his pocket before she had a chance to reply.

Jason. Finally.

West swiped the screen and pressed the phone to his ear. "Talk to me. What's going on there? How's Shane?"

"Shane's doing well. He's awake and talking to his parents. The doctors are going to keep him for three or four days but then he can go home with a health nurse to care for him. He told me to tell you not to worry and take care of your girl."

West breathed out a heavy sigh of relief. The surgery had gone on longer than planned and his cousin had been in the recovery room for what seemed like hours.

"That's good news. I bet he's loving all the attention," West laughed, remembering Shane's predilection for dating pretty nurses. "Tell him we're thinking about him, okay?"

"I will. But that's not all the good news I have. I finally got that call back from my buddy in the FBI. He's been working on the Morton case for over two years now and he's willing to help us. Says that good old Alan is as dirty as they come. Gambling. Prostitution. Drugs. A veritable trifecta of sins."

"Do they have enough to make a case?"

"They've got some circumstantial stuff but he'd like to get a slam dunk for the prosecutor. Morton hasn't been a high priority yet, honestly. They've been using him to get to targets higher up."

Adrenaline raced through West's veins at the thought of putting Morton behind bars for the rest of the man's miserable life. "Whatever we can do to expedite this I'm all for. I want this guy. Bad."

"I know," Jason grunted. "We'll get him. Now I'm going to stay with Shane but Travis and Jared can fly down and meet you in Vegas if you need them. There's nothing they can really do here but sit around and watch Shane terrorize the nurses and generally make everyone's life miserable. I can already tell he's going to be a piss poor patient."

All the Anderson men were cursed with little patience. In a few days Shane was going to chafe at having to lie in a hospital bed.

"I'll call you later today after Gigi meets her brother. I'll have a better idea at that point when we'll be leaving for Chicago."

"Sounds good. I'll be talking to my buddy again and finding out his plans for Morton. Maybe we can help out."

Anything that removed Morton from Gigi's life was okay with West.

"Let me know." West ended the call and slid the phone back

in his pocket. "Shane is going to be okay. He said not to worry about him and to take care of business."

Gigi closed her eyes as if saying a prayer of thanks. "I'm so glad. I haven't been able to think of much else."

"You've got way too many things to worry about these days. Let's see if we can remove at least one of them."

West pointed to Wyatt who was striding toward their truck, a smile on his face. The meeting with Zach must have gone well. It was time to reunite the woman West loved with her brother. After all these years she'd finally have a family.

There wasn't anything West wouldn't give to Gigi if it was in his power.

Chapter Seventeen

O N TREMBLING LEGS Gigi walked into the building, her gaze scanning from left to right. A large red mat covered about two-thirds of the floor and the walls were adorned with floor to ceiling mirrors all around. Boxing gloves and pads were stacked on shelving at one end while heavy bags for punching and kicking were positioned in a corner.

The room contained one lone man. Tall with broad shoulders and golden brown hair he stood motionless, his gaze trained on her, seeking and hopeful. She'd changed over the years and perhaps he wouldn't recognize her. Maybe he'd forgotten her and Aubrey.

She would have known his handsome face anywhere.

He broke into a smile and he took two large strides, wrapping her into his strong embrace.

"Gigi. My Gigi."

His voice broke with emotion and she hiccupped, trying to keep from crying. Again. It was starting to feel like all she did these days but she couldn't hold back the tidal wave of love she felt for this big strong man even after all this time. He was her brother. Her protector.

Her throat tightened painfully and she managed to croak out his name, burying her face in his chest. His arms were rocking her as they both cried, this reunion too long in the making. After several minutes he reluctantly pulled back and wiped at her cheeks.

"I was beginning to think I'd never see you again, little sis. I've been looking for you for so damn long. But I never gave up hope. Wyatt said you never did either."

"Never." Gigi shook her head, his face blurred from her tears. "I can't believe this is really happening. It just seems so surreal."

He pulled her in for another bear hug. "It's real, alright. I can't wait to hear about your life. No detail is too small. I want to know every single thing about what you've been doing and who you've become. What are your favorite books? What's your favorite food? Do you still hate thunderstorms?"

"All the Harry Potter books. Pizza. And yes, I still hate storms. They're scary. I was so glad to have you there when the thunder and lightning got too bad. I always knew you would protect me."

Zach glanced behind her where West was standing. "Is that who protects you now? Is he your husband?"

Zach had kept his voice low but Gigi had a feeling West still heard the "husband" remark. Her cheeks grew warm at the implied intimacy she wasn't sure she – or West – was ready for and she tried to cover her embarrassment with a cough.

"That's West Anderson, my…boyfriend." Shit, she didn't even know what to call him. This was pathetic. "He's been helping me…"

Her voice trailed off, not sure how to begin telling her big brother how her life was so crazy she needed bodyguards.

Zach's gaze shifted from her to West and back to her. "Well, that's good then. Are you going to introduce me?"

"Of course." She tugged on Zach's hand and West came to stand by her, his arm around her waist. "West, this is my brother Zach. Zach, this is West."

The men shook hands, clearly sizing each other up. Something good must have passed between them – or maybe they'd squeezed the ever loving crap out of each other's fingers – but they seemed to relax, their smiles easier and more genuine.

"It's good to finally meet you, Zach. Gigi's told me so much about you. And her sister, Aubrey."

Zach's face split into a mile wide grin. "I got so distracted I almost forgot to tell you. I got a call from Aubrey this morning. She found me. Isn't that amazing? I found both my sisters practically at the same time. She's still in Chicago."

West's brows shot up and he glanced back to Wyatt, who was guarding the entrance but could hear everything being said. "That is amazing. What are the odds? Chicago, you said?"

"Yes, I told her I'd come visit her. Maybe we can all go." Zach shook his head, his hand still holding her own. "I guess I probably sound pushy but I'm just so damn happy to have my family back. This has been the best day of my life."

"Me too," Gigi said, meaning it more than she could express with mere words. She still hadn't dealt with West's declaration in the truck earlier regarding his love for her, but her doubt about that relationship didn't diminish her excitement about finding her brother.

She'd deal with West and his love later. When she could think more clearly. He'd thrown down the gauntlet, issuing an ultimatum, and she wasn't sure how she felt about that either. Having been on her own for most of her life she didn't take kindly to a man laying down the law about anything, let alone about her future.

"I need to finish up here but why don't we go to lunch and we can talk? Really talk. What do you think?"

Gigi looked up at West and he nodded his head.

"That sounds good. You know this area—what do you suggest?"

If Zach thought it was strange that she needed West's approval to go to lunch he didn't say so. "There's a really good Italian place just a few blocks down. I just need about fifteen minutes. If you want you can go ahead and get a table and I'll follow you. It can get busy this time of day."

"We can do that. Where is it located?" West asked, checking his phone. He was waiting for more news from Jason about the agent who would help them put Alan behind bars.

Zach gave them directions and she hugged her brother one more time before they exited the building, her heart still pounding in her chest.

She'd found Zach. And Aubrey too. After years of it being just her she was no longer alone.

It felt strange. But good. Gigi had a family that loved her. West said he did too.

Everything had changed but it didn't feel quite real.

She had to believe in it. And that was the hardest part.

✦   ✦   ✦

WEST PULLED WYATT aside as Gigi and Zach chatted away at a corner table in the Italian restaurant. The food was as good as Zach had promised and the newly reunited brother and sister had spent the last hour catching up on their lives.

Unmentioned so far?

Gigi's control-freak stalker ex-boyfriend and Zach's life since leaving the military. He'd told her all about his years with a foster family that had eventually adopted him. He'd also talked about his time in the Middle East but he'd pretty much stopped talking at the point of his discharge.

West and Wyatt stood by the swinging kitchen door, far enough away that they wouldn't be overheard by Gigi and Zach. The place was busy and between the chatter of diners and the tinkling of silverware they hadn't had to move far.

"Did you hear Zach earlier? Sister Aubrey just happens to get in touch with him, today of all days. I'm getting a hinky vibe about this."

Wyatt nodded grimly, his lips a flat line. "If I were in your shoes I wouldn't like it at all. What do you know about this sister? Could she be working with this Morton character? It's just too much of a coincidence for me."

"I'll have a friend of mine look into her past. Now that we know she's in Chicago and that she has a new last name he should be able to find out what she's been doing all these years."

"Do you think it's a trap?"

West laughed but the situation wasn't remotely funny. "Yes, but I don't think we have any choice. There's no way I'm going to talk Gigi out of seeing her sister and we need to go to Chicago to meet up with Jason's agent friend if we want Morton behind bars. It doesn't leave me many options."

Wyatt jaw tightened, a dangerous glint in his eyes. "I can go with you if you want. Never been to Chicago."

"Are you sure?" Wyatt hadn't been over a hundred miles from his house in over three years. "I could use the help but I know you don't like traveling or being away from home."

His friend rubbed his chin and grimaced. "About that...I think maybe I've been a hermit for too long. I should get out more. Live a little. Hell, if Gigi can leave her home every day with a madman trying to turn her into some sort of pet or plaything the very least I can do is drag my ass out of the house. No one's trying to kill me." Wyatt grinned. "At least I don't think they are. I could be wrong. There was that high-stakes card game in Tijuana."

Wyatt had a world class poker face. He could have gone professional if he'd had ambitions in that direction. "Then I accept your offer with gratitude. I'll call Jason and have him and Jared meet us in in Chicago. No sense them coming all the way down here when we're just going to up and leave."

"Got a plan for this trip?" Wyatt arched an eyebrow.

"Nope, but it's early yet." West grinned. "We haven't seen any of Morton's men, but if Morton had Aubrey call Zach then he has to know we're here. We need to assume he'll come at us."

And West would need to be ready.

Chapter Eighteen

"SO YOU WORK in a karate studio? That sounds like fun."

Gigi sipped her iced tea, her gaze fixed to Zach and still amazed he was sitting across from her eating a large plate of ziti. He resembled Aubrey more than Gigi with his long legs, light brown hair, and blue eyes. Their mother had always said Gigi got her blonde hair from her grandmother and Zach and Aubrey got their brown hair from their grandfather. Gigi had never met any of her mother's family so she didn't know if it was true or not.

"Actually it's mixed martial arts, which is very different. It takes the best techniques from several disciplines. My job is to run classes for the kids and I also help coach the fight team."

One look at Zach and anyone could see he was in fantastic shape. "How did you end up here in Vegas?"

Her brother shrugged nonchalantly but his shoulders stiffened. "An old friend runs the gym. He offered me a job so here I am. I'd never been to Vegas so it seemed like a good idea at the time."

"Meaning it's not now?"

Her gaze searched his expression for clues. He'd spoken easily of their years apart until now. He didn't seem to want to talk about his recent past.

"It's okay. It's a job and I needed one."

She knew all about that. "I can relate. I've moved around for the last few years. Mostly I wait tables or tend bar. I think about going to college but maybe I'm too old."

Or in danger.

"You're not even thirty, sis. What would you study if you could go back?"

"I'd like to help kids like us. I was thinking I might enjoy being a social worker."

Zach reached across the table and patted her hand. "You always were a soft touch. I imagine you would be quite good at it. If you want to do that what are you waiting for?"

She'd never intended to lie to him about the last few years but she'd underestimated how difficult it would be to tell him. Telling West had been hard enough, but then he'd been incredibly pissed off at the time while Zach had no idea the implications of the question he'd asked.

"Well…it's funny you asked that. The last few years have been challenging to say the least. You suggested we travel to Chicago together to see Aubrey so there's something you should know before we go."

His fingers tightened on her own and his smile fell. "I'm listening. Is everything okay?"

West and Wyatt chose that moment to join them at the table. West's gaze flickered back and forth between Gigi and Zach. "Did we interrupt?"

Gigi shook her head, her stomach clenching painfully. Zach

was going to think she was a complete idiot.

He might not want to be around her anymore once he found out Alan wanted her under his thumb. Or dead. Alan also wanted anyone around her dead which wasn't good news for Zach. He might decide it was more prudent to walk away until her life was pieced back together. She wouldn't blame him a bit.

"I was just about to tell Zach about Alan," she said softly. "He needs to know."

No matter what it cost her it was time to face her past and move on. Alan didn't get to win. Not anymore.

✦   ✦   ✦

"I THINK WE'RE being followed."

Zach had pulled West aside as they'd headed toward the elevators of their hotel. Lunch was over and Gigi had told her story. Her brother had alternated between anger at Morton and sympathy for his sister. Zach had muttered something under his breath about kicking Morton's ass but he'd have to get in line. West wanted to do it himself.

West didn't even glance over his shoulder. "I think you're right, although how you knew I'd like to know. They're not doing too bad a job of it."

A smile slowly spread across Zach's face. At that moment he looked very much like Gigi.

"I told you I was in the military and that I've done some private security as well. I was a bodyguard for a couple of hotshot movie actors. They've got females following them in droves and they're always trying to sneak up into the hotel room for some naked action. After awhile you get a sixth sense about it."

"I don't think these guys want to get naked," West chuckled. "But I do think they'd like to get their hands on Gigi. I don't intend to let that happen. They'll have to go through me first."

"And me," declared Zach, his jaw tight. "I haven't met this guy Alan but already I think he's slime."

West and Zach were going to get along fine.

"He is slime. Some of the worst. Gambling. Drugs. Prostitution. And those are his good qualities. The rest of the time he's a controlling asshole who wants to turn Gigi into a life-size Barbie doll."

Zach glanced at Gigi talking animatedly to Wyatt near a magazine display. "If I'd been around none of this would have happened. I should have been there."

Gigi had mentioned Zach had a protective streak a mile wide but it was no time for ifs, ands, or buts. The past was the past and they needed to focus on the present. They were far from out of the woods.

"Don't beat yourself up about it. What matters is that you and Gigi can be a family again."

Zach nodded absently, his mind somewhere else. "I want to help."

"Help? I'm not sure I follow you."

"I want to help you get him. I want to help keep her safe."

"I know you mean well but this could get danger—"

"Fuck that." Zach angrily waved away West's warning. "I've been in combat. I've been a bodyguard. I've got a black belt. Shit, I can handle myself."

West rubbed the back of his neck and sighed. "If you get hurt Gigi will kill me."

Zach laughed and slapped West on the shoulder. "You're not afraid of a little bitty thing like her, are you? Man up, my friend."

West quirked an eyebrow. Clearly Zach had been separated from Gigi for too long. "Your sister has been on her own for a long time and she can handle herself too. She's a damn good shot and not bad in hand to hand combat. She wouldn't hesitate to knee me, and you, in the balls so watch yourself."

"I'll gird my loins. So are you going to let me help or not? I don't see that you have much choice really with only Wyatt to help you."

West hated it when other people were right. He needed Zach and the man did look like a freaking brick wall.

"You can help but just so we're clear about the chain of command...I'm in charge. Got it?"

Zach's brows shot up but he didn't object. "Got it. Does the man in charge have any ideas as to how we're going to get to Chicago without being followed?"

Shit. Fuck.

"No," West admitted. "My training says to create a diversion but that's as far as I've gotten with the plan."

"You're in luck," Zach grinned. "I have an idea. Want to hear it?"

"I'm open to any and all ideas. Let's head to the hotel room."

West led the way upstairs with Wyatt and Zach surrounding Gigi. Someone was watching them and the sooner West shook the tail the better. Whatever was waiting for them in Chicago didn't need to know the minute Gigi stepped foot in the city.

Time for a covert operation.

Chapter Nineteen

GIGI FLIPPED THROUGH the television channels one by one but not really paying any attention to the screen. They'd ordered room service and had dinner with Zach and Wyatt. Pizza and a bottle of Chianti which had made Gigi slightly dizzy. West had teased her and said she was a cheap date. One drink and she was feeling it.

"Are you even watching the TV?"

West stood next to the bed wearing nothing but an unzipped pair of blue jeans and a smile that showed off that dimple in his cheek. Despite all the crap they'd been through in the last few days her libido perked up and took notice of his very fine self. There ought to be a law against a man being that damn sexy, but then he'd probably just charm his way out of jail.

Drop dead gorgeous.

Gigi would never admit it out loud but she was attracted to men with an edge. Alan's edginess had been a cover for someone who was deeply and irrevocably disturbed. A violent man, he couldn't control the demons that drove him to do unspeakable acts upon other human beings.

West, on the other hand, had an aura of strength about him.

He was an alpha male that others rarely messed with since he carried himself with such incredible confidence. It wasn't arrogance either, but some innate quality that made men want to follow him into battle and women want to take his pants off.

As a young woman Gigi hadn't been able to discern the difference between a violent, controlling asshole and a swaggering, cocksure but protective male. Thankfully this time she'd finally found the right man.

A man that loved her and had basically demanded she love him back. Period.

Love was a word she hadn't used much in her life. She adored West. She wanted him around all the time and she couldn't imagine her life without him. She trusted him. Wanted to make love to him. Wanted to laugh and joke around. She even liked it when they simply sat around and watched a movie.

Was that love?

If so she was screwed because he evoked such strong emotions she didn't even have words to describe them anymore. He was West and he was all she needed.

She hit the off button on the remote and tossed it aside. "No, I'm not really watching television. I'm thinking about tomorrow. Tell me again why we're flying and not driving."

"Because we're being followed," West explained patiently. "We'll shake the tail and fly to Chicago. Since we've been driving all this time they won't expect that. I want the element of surprise on our side."

West had impressed upon her that they needed every advantage they could get. Alan would be waiting there with some evil plot to take her away.

"And just how are you going to get Alan's men off our tail? If they know we're here in the hotel they'll be waiting for us to leave."

West chuckled and leaned against the dresser, his long legs stretched out. "I'm counting on that. Now are you done asking questions? Just trust me, babe. I feel good about this plan. I promised I'd get you to your brother and I did. Now I promise I'll get you to Chicago and your sister."

He was a man who kept his promises. It was one of the reasons she'd been with him this long.

"I am done and I do trust you. So we just sit tight until morning?"

She doubted she'd get much sleep with more traveling the next day. She longed to curl up in West's bed, his body pressed against her own. She would sleep for days.

"I have something else in mind. You've been under so much stress. You need to relax. I thought a date night might do the trick."

West had that sneaky look she knew so well. Shit eating grin. Twinkling green eyes. Her man was in the mood to be naughty.

And she was a lucky girl.

"How are we going to go out on a date? I heard you tell Wyatt that we were in for the night."

Wyatt was staying in a connecting room and there was only an unlocked door separating them in case something happened.

"We are in for the night but he gave me a hand with the set-up." West opened the small refrigerator and pulled out a bottle. "Champagne to start us off."

Gigi laughed as West popped the bottle open and the golden

liquid fizzed over the top. He poured a little into two plastic cups and handed her one. "I never knew you were so romantic, Westin Anderson. I'm impressed."

"There's a lot of things you don't know about me. You should stick around and discover them all. How about a toast? To us." He leaned down, one hand on the bed so their gazes met. Her heart accelerated in her chest at his intense but passionate expression. "And to our future."

With a shaky hand she lifted the cup and tapped his own. He wasn't going to let up on her. "To us and the future."

She sipped the tart liquid, the bubbles tickling her nose and making her sneeze and giggle. "This is good. I could get used to drinking champagne in Las Vegas."

West had expressed his regret that they weren't able to truly enjoy being in Sin City and had promised a future trip to make up for this one. She could have cared less, honestly. Being with him was quite enough. Only a few days ago she'd thought she'd never see him again.

"I'm just sorry we're not here for a better reason." He set his cup down and dug into his bag and pulled out his iPod. "Champagne is only the beginning. There's also dancing."

He placed the player onto the clock radio dock and the slow strains of *At This Moment* filled the room. Holding out his hand, he gave her a sexy smile and showed off that dimple. "Come dance with me, babe. Let me try and help you forget everything but the two of us."

He was better at that than he knew. Whenever she was in his arms it was as if the world fell away. But she always seemed to come down to earth with a jolt. Reality could be highly overrated at times.

They seemed to float together, her feet never quite touching the ground. His body brushed hers, sending sparks straight to her core. Her heart raced and her knees trembled at his nearness, his warm citrusy scent teasing her nostrils. It was a solid, manly aroma that wrapped around her like the softest comforter. When she was with West the fear that she'd lived with for so long melted like ice on a hot day.

Speaking of heat…

What had begun as a slow simmer of warmth in her abdomen had turned into a five-alarm barn burner that had her pressing herself as close as she could get to West's muscular frame. Arousal pooled in her belly and her nails dug into his biceps when he dipped his head and slid his lips along the cord of her neck. She moaned and quaked, her eyelids fluttering closed to savor the ricocheting sensations that were currently making her world spin.

Cool air between them caused her eyes to snap open. West had taken a step back and was regarding her steadily, a deep vee between his brows.

"What's your favorite movie?"

Gigi had to shake her head to loosen the cobwebs. "What? I don't understand."

She'd thought they'd been about to make love but he wanted to play Twenty Questions instead?

"What's your favorite movie?" he pressed, an exasperated look on his handsome face. "This always happens. I start out with the best of intentions to find out more about you and then we end up in bed. I won't let that happen this time. Dammit, woman, I was trying to be romantic."

Gigi tilted her head in question. He seemed completely serious. He wanted to know her favorite movie instead of having sex.

Well...okay.

"*Rear Window.* It's a Hitchcock film with Grace Kelly and Jimmy Stewart."

His frown only deepened. "I know that. I saw it years ago."

If he wanted to discuss film she could do that, although she could think of far more pleasurable things to be doing. "It's a cinematic masterpiece. The first five minutes of the film not a word is spoken but Hitchcock communicates the setting and circumstances perfectly."

"Are you a big Hitchcock fan?"

This entire conversation was surreal. Her body was humming and she could clearly see the bulge in his pants but they were talking about movies.

What the hell?

"I wouldn't say I'm a big fan. I liked *Dial M for Murder* and I thought *Psycho* was scarier than hell but some of his other films were just so-so for me."

"*Psycho* was scary. We should watch it together sometime. What's your favorite color?"

Apparently they weren't done.

"Red. Next question."

"I should have known that." His lips twisted and he nodded. "You wear a lot of red. What's your favorite ice cream flavor?"

"Chocolate marshmallow. Are we done now? Because the mood is rapidly dissipating, West."

He crossed his arms over his broad chest. "I told myself that I'd get to know you. Really know you. I don't want us to get distracted."

West was a wonderfully sweet man but he simply didn't understand. How could he not see something that was so incredibly clear to her?

"You know me better than anyone in the world," she said simply. "You may not know my favorite foods or where the scar on my knee came from but you know me. You know the me inside."

His gaze flickered down to her leg but they were covered in denim. "How did you get that scar on your knee?"

Gigi smiled at the memory. "We were at the park and Zach was pushing me on the swing. I kept telling him I wanted to go higher and higher and he kept pushing me harder and harder. The inevitable happened and somehow I let go of the chains holding up the swing. I flew several feet and cut my knee on a rock."

His expression softened and he reached out to run his rough fingers down her cheek, sending a streak of arousal straight through her. "I bet that hurt. Did you cry?"

"I tried not to but yeah, I did. Zach cleaned me up and put a band-aid on it but now I have a little reminder of that day."

"I want to know everything about you." His voice was soft but there was a tinge of frustration in the tone. Typical West Anderson. Most things in his life had come quickly and easily so he thought this should too. She'd already let him in further than she'd ever planned.

"You will...eventually, I'm guessing. But you already know

the important things. Everything else is just details."

"What do you think is important?"

She sat down on the bed and let her mind wander back over the last three months with him. The time they'd spent together had been some of the happiest of her life, despite all the crap she'd had to hide from him.

"You know my mood just by looking at me. Even when I'm trying to hide it. You know how to make me laugh. I especially like it when you do the Kermit the Frog voice. It cracks me up every single time. That always makes my day no matter how bad it's been."

His face flushed at the mention of his Muppet impressions. For a sex god he was kind of dorky once someone got to know him.

"I like making you laugh. You didn't do much of it when we first met so I might have acted a little silly in the beginning. You know, to see you smile."

Gigi clapped a hand over her mouth, emotion tightening her chest. If he only knew how much that meant to her. No one had gone out of their way like that just to see her smile. "And no one tells worse jokes than you do. Some of them are truly bad. Like the horse that walked into the bar and the bartender said–"

"Hey buddy, why the long face?" West finished for her, a grin spreading across his own face. "That's a great joke."

"It's a silly joke," she giggled. "But that's just part of all the things you know. You knew, even when I didn't tell you, that I had a secret. You never gave up on me. You saw something inside of me I didn't even see myself."

West was looking at her like she was the greatest thing in the world. Why hadn't she noticed it before? It was the same way she looked at him.

"Love."

Tears stung the back of her eyes and she had to blink several times to keep them from sliding down her cheeks. She was tired of fucking crying.

"Love," she agreed. "I didn't think I had any left inside of me. I thought fear had taken up all the space in my heart. But you simply wouldn't take no for an answer."

"You love me."

It wasn't a question and she didn't argue the validity of the statement. Its truth was so deep she couldn't deny it. She owed him that and more. From now on no more half-truths or evasions. Honesty was the only path she'd follow. She loved him.

There, she'd said it. Or at least thought it. Saying the words out loud was terrifying.

"I do. I think I have for a while now." She held up her hand when he would have moved toward her. "But it doesn't solve anything. I'm still kind of messed up from my childhood and Alan is still hanging over our heads."

"He won't be for long." West looked every inch the confident lawman that he was. "We'll get him. You need to start thinking about the kind of future you want. And who you want to be part of it."

Until the last few days she'd never allowed herself to think about the future but the possibility of being truly free seemed finally within her grasp. Having West there would be sheer heaven.

"I'm not trying to evade the question. I'm honestly having

trouble realizing that this entire nightmare might be over soon. I've never been that lucky in my life."

"Your luck is about to change, babe. If I have anything to say about it, anyway. Are you open to having me in your life? Do you love me enough to give us a shot?"

She hadn't wanted to but she did. Exhausted from fighting her growing feelings for this man, she didn't play games or pretend. The time for that had past. "Yes. But I'm scared to death. I don't know that I know how to do this."

West reached down and popped the button on his jeans, a wicked grin crossing his face. "You know, I've never been in a serious relationship either so we'll have to learn together. But I do know one thing we're damn good at."

Finally. She'd been worried her horndog man didn't find her attractive anymore.

Those sinfully well-fitting blue jeans slid down his muscled thighs before he kicked them aside. His hard length sprung free, slapping his flat abdomen and she simply couldn't keep her hands to herself. She reached out and wrapped her fingers around the thick shaft, exploring every ridge and curve. West hissed his approval and closed his eyes to savor every sensation and caress.

His unbridled response made her bold and she leaned forward to give his cock a lick, her tongue running around the head before sliding up and down the shaft until his breathing was ragged and his fingers were tangled in her hair.

"Easy, babe. I've got much more in mind."

She had a few rather dirty thoughts as well.

Gigi pressed a kiss to his hip bone and then traced circles

around his belly button with her tongue.

"Then what are you waiting for, handsome? I'm all yours."

Man, was she ever. No one had ever made her feel all quivery the way West did. He had her panting his name with just a few flicks of that talented tongue.

"You're wearing too many clothes." His hands tugged at the skimpy tank top she'd paired with a pair of striped cotton sleep shorts. "Get naked, woman."

She loved hearing the note of impatience in his voice, especially since she felt exactly the same. West tossed her top away as she slipped out of her shorts, kicking them across the room to land on her suitcase.

Giggling, she ran her fingers up his chest, exploring all the dips and planes of his body and drawing a ragged groan from his lips. She couldn't get enough of touching him, his body endlessly fascinating. Finding new spots that brought him pleasure was a wonderful way to pass the time.

"You're a naughty woman," West growled but a smile played on his well-shaped lips. "I think you need a spanking."

It was a running joke between them. He threatened to spank her and she threatened to kick him in the balls if he did. Although the longer they kept laughing about it, the more Gigi kind of wanted him to do it. Maybe. It sounded hot and sexy.

She blew a raspberry and rolled her eyes. "Conan the Barbarian speaks. I doubt you've got the stones, honestly."

West's eyes lit up at the challenge as she'd known they would. She knew how to get his motor running and a little friendly competition would send his libido into orbit.

"You're playing with fire, little girl. Are you sure you want to do that?"

His head dipped down and captured a nipple in his mouth, sucking and licking until she was writhing underneath his massive frame.

"Just fuck me," she breathed. "Give it to me, you asshole."

"Tsk, tsk, such language for a lady. I think you definitely need to be taught a lesson."

Gigi saw him move a second before he did. She lunged for the other side of the bed but his fingers landed around her ankle, dragging her back across the mattress. How she could be this turned on and still laughing her ass off she didn't know, but her giggles completely ceased when his palm came smartly down on her bottom.

Yelping at the indignity, she clawed at the sheets to get away but his hand came down on her ass cheek once again, leaving a searing heat in its wake. She twisted around to tell him off but the fire from her ass was already traveling straight to her slit. Arousal coiled tightly in her belly and she opened her mouth to protest but his kiss obliterated any coherent thoughts she might have left.

His warm lips traveled down her neck between her breasts and over her belly, nipping and licking at the wet trail he'd created. His tongue snaked out and traced a line along her inner thigh and she moaned when he hit a most sensitive spot behind her knee.

"I see you've stopped calling me names," West teased as he blew on her clit, sending frissons of pleasure zipping through her veins. "That's progress. But now I think we need to get serious about this. You need to come for me, babe."

Flames licked at her flesh as he did wonderfully evil things with his tongue. Her entire being was consumed with white hot heat as he closed his lips over her clit, his teeth lightly scraping the sensitive bud.

"Now."

Her body never failed to respond to that deep, dark, *I am God* tone. Her orgasm exploded like fireworks on the Fourth of July. Multi-colored lights danced behind her lids and her toes curled, leaving her struggling for breath. Breathless and deliriously happy. At that moment she wasn't sure why they didn't do this every single day at least three or four times.

His hard body covered hers and he nudged at her entrance. Clinging to him like a boat in a storm, she panted as he pressed forward, so wet he easily slid into the hilt.

"Open your eyes. I want you to see me."

Forcing her eyes open she drank in the man before her looking down at her with so much love and lust, more than she'd ever dreamed. Their gazes locked as he began to move slowly at first and then faster, harder. Each thrust rubbed sensitive spots inside her that only he had ever found. She dug her nails into his shoulders as her arousal moved higher, teetering on the precipice of another climax.

West grunted, sweat forming on his forehead. His jaw clenched tightly with the effort of holding back his own completion. Always the gentleman, he was waiting for her.

Grinding against him with each stroke she fell over the cliff, his name on her lips. She hovered in the shimmering sky far above the earth, floating and flying until she finally came down from her perch in heaven, still smiling with perfect contentment.

West had also reached the pinnacle and was now lying heavily on top of her, his breathing labored and his skin damp from exertion. She ran her hands down his spine delighting in the shiver of response she felt under her fingers. His lips found the sensitive spot where her neck and shoulder met before rolling over onto his back. Taking her with him West tucked her into his side, his face covered in a grin of pure male satisfaction.

"Get some rest because I'm going to want to do that again in a few hours."

His tone was teasing but his sexual appetite was no joke. He was totally serious.

"You're the horniest man I've ever met, West Anderson."

Not that she'd known that many but he didn't need every single detail of her sexual history. His ego was already two sizes too big most days. He didn't lack self-esteem.

Lying on his chest she felt his chuckle under her ear, a low rumble in his chest. "If I thought you meant that as anything but a compliment I'd be worried but you love it. Admit it, Gigi. You love that I chase you around the bedroom panting after you. You love that I can't get enough."

She'd promised herself not to keep secrets from him anymore.

Dammit.

"It's not your worst trait," she finally conceded, smiling up at him. "But if you're thinking round two we really do need to get some rest. We have a big day tomorrow."

For the first time in two years she was going back to Chicago. She would probably see Alan at some point. It shouldn't scare her...but it did.

Somehow West must have sensed her thoughts.

"Then close your eyes and sleep. I'll be right here by your side all night."

All night. Maybe forever. If she wanted a life with West it all started with her. Burying the past and getting over her love and family issues. If she wasn't careful she'd lose the best thing that had ever happened to her.

Chapter Twenty

WEST CHECKED THE hotel room for anything they might have forgotten to pack. Still dark outside, it was time to go to the airport. Wyatt and Zach were in the next room, the countdown begun. Dressed but still sleepy, Gigi yawned widely, taking another sip of her coffee. West had woken her at two in the morning and she'd kicked up quite the fuss. He hadn't told her how early they were leaving on purpose. He hadn't wanted her to be nervous and then not be able to sleep. As it was he hadn't slept much, his mind on the plan that he, Zach, and Wyatt had put together. He needed to get Gigi safely to the airport despite the fact that Morton's henchmen were breathing down their neck.

The next ten minutes would make or break the entire trip to Chicago. Plan B sucked so this had to be right. No second chances.

"How are we going to get out of here without Alan's men seeing us?"

West hadn't told her much up to now but the time had come. The adrenaline pumped through his veins and he tugged at the suddenly too tight collar of his button-down shirt. Out of all the missions he'd been on in the Middle East and then on the Tremont police force this one meant the most.

"I want his men to see us. I need for them to believe we're leaving the hotel and getting on the road."

"We *are* leaving the hotel and getting on the road. Or haven't I had enough of this yet?" Gigi held up her coffee cup. "Your plan is to let them follow us?"

West knocked twice on the connecting door and then slid it open. "No, the plan is to let Morton's men follow *them*."

Zach, Wyatt, and a young blonde woman walked into the room. West held out his hand to the female who had agreed to help them. "I'm West Anderson and this is Gigi Sidney. I want to thank you for helping us this morning. We couldn't do this without you."

She shook his hand and smiled. "I'm Shiloh Harper, a friend of Zach's and I'm glad I could help." Gigi had stood and the two women also shook hands. "Looks like we're about the same size. This might just work."

Zach gave his sister a hug and a smile. "You look confused, Sis. You and Shiloh are going to switch places. She and Wyatt are going to pretend to be you and West. They'll get in Wyatt's truck and head toward the highway. In the meantime you, me, and West will hightail it to the airport to catch a flight to Chicago. Hopefully leaving in the dark will help with our little sleight of hand. Now you need to switch jackets with Shiloh."

Gigi looked confused at first but then realization dawned and she quickly shrugged out of her red hoodie, exchanging it for Shiloh's blue windbreaker. Morton's men would expect West and Gigi to try and disguise themselves to sneak out of the hotel so Zach had purchased hats and sunglasses that were as conspicuous as Gigi's scarlet jacket. Hopefully Wyatt and Shiloh would garner all of the attention leaving Zach, West, and Gigi to zip to the airport under the radar.

"You two will also be switching luggage and purses. Basically anything that is distinctive about you."

Gigi pointed down to her pink Converse tennis shoes, a glum expression on her face. They were worn and ought to be tossed in the trash but he knew how much she loved them. "These too?"

"I'll buy you another pair, I promise, but yes, those too."

The women made quick work of exchanging shoes and bags. Shiloh's feet were slightly larger than Gigi's and she winced a little as she shoved her feet into the sneaker. Gigi, on the other hand, had to lace her shoes tightly to keep them from falling off. Gigi's clothes moved from her own suitcase to an empty one Zach had brought with him, and then purse contents made the journey from one bag to the other. Gigi's handbag was weighed down with miscellaneous items that West had no idea why she carried. Maybe years of being on the run gave her the habit of toting around a good portion of her worldly possessions.

West shook hands with Wyatt, giving him thanks for all he'd done. As was his habit he'd gone above and beyond anything West could have expected.

"I owe you."

Wyatt shook his head and donned the hat and sunglasses. "This just makes us even. You've done the same for me. Just keep Gigi safe and get that asshole, okay? We'll take care of his evil minions."

Wyatt's shoulder holster was hidden by his coat and Shiloh had a handgun tucked in under her hoodie. Zach had assured West that Shiloh was a martial arts expert and could handle herself if things got ugly. They'd be fine but what they were doing was still dangerous.

Hell, taking Gigi to the airport wasn't the safest thing he'd ever done but he had little choice.

It was time.

✦   ✦   ✦

GIGI PULLED UP the collar of the borrowed windbreaker and shivered, not from a chill but from anticipation mixed with a healthy dose of fear. Wyatt and Shiloh had made their way out of the hotel and were currently standing in front of the entrance, waiting for the valet to bring their vehicle. Meanwhile she, Zach, and West were sitting in the room waiting for Wyatt to call them when they were on the road, hopefully with some company in tow.

Sitting on the bed Gigi tried to wait patiently for the signal that it was safe to leave the hotel. Zach and West were standing near the window, looking down at the street below but not saying a word. The silence in the room collided with the screaming voices inside her head, making her temples ache. The tension in the room was thick and she took a sip from her coffee, her hands shaking.

"Time to go," West announced, his gaze trained on his phone. "They're on the road and Wyatt thinks they've picked up a tail."

Not realizing she'd been holding her breath Gigi slowly exhaled, relief flooding her insides that had moments before been twisted into sailing knots. They weren't in the clear but the first step was in motion.

Gigi pulled up the hood of the windbreaker so that it covered most of her face while Zach and West donned baseball caps. Slinging Shiloh's purse over her shoulder, Gigi grabbed the suitcase with her belongings but Zach eased it from her tense fingers.

"I got this, Sis. Just stay in between us and keep your head down."

Heart hammering in her chest, she did just that as they exited the room and walked at a leisurely pace down the hallway to the bank of elevators. Just three people out for a stroll in a twenty-four-seven city filled with gambling, liquor, and other assorted vices.

Nothing to see here, folks. Move along.

At this time of the morning there was no one else waiting for the elevator so they slipped down to the lobby alone, their speed picking up as they approached the front doors.

"Grab the yellow taxi. They all look alike and we'll get lost in the traffic," Zach said softly.

He knew the city so neither Gigi nor West argued, simply nodding in agreement. In less than a minute the three of them were sitting in the back of a cab headed straight for the airport. Step two was now also complete. Just a million more to go.

Gigi rubbed her forehead where a tiny hammer was currently pounding up a storm. "Are we being followed? Did they leave someone back in case that wasn't us earlier?"

West had twisted around in his seat to look out the back

window. "If they buy into Shiloh and Wyatt it wouldn't make any sense to leave someone behind. But if they figured out that it was a diversion then yes, we could be followed."

He turned forward and rubbed the back of his neck. There were circles under his eyes that clearly illustrated the lack of sleep since she'd shared her tale of woe with him. He'd taken all of her problems onto his own shoulders and the burden was heavy. For him it was life and death. For her it was a spiritual rather than physical demise. She could never allow herself to be Alan's prisoner again.

The streets were surprisingly busy despite the early hour in the morning but the taxi zipped through the traffic without incident. The vehicle pulled up to the departures entrance at three-fifteen on the dot. They were intentionally cutting it close, not wanting to mill about the airport. The flight was scheduled to leave in forty-five minutes and they still needed to check in. Luckily there were only a few people in line ahead of them.

Gigi tried not to act suspiciously but she couldn't help the furtive glances over her shoulder, looking for one of Alan's men out of the corner of her eye. Everyone looked threatening and her nervousness must have shown on her face because West placed his hand on her shoulder, giving it a comforting squeeze.

"Relax. Zach and I are watching everyone and everything. I'm not going to let anything happen to you."

"I know," Gigi murmured, training her gaze forward. "I just wish we were on the airplane. Then I can relax."

"I won't relax until Morton is behind bars," West growled as they stepped up to the check in counter. "I don't want you to worry but I also want you to be vigilant."

Did he actually say that?

They walked away from the counter and she elbowed him in the ribs. "Please don't forget that I've spent the last two years being vigilant. I think I know how much I can allow myself to relax without getting myself killed."

The words had come out bitchier than she'd intended but her nerves were stretched to the limit. Palms sweaty. Aching headache. Tumbling stomach. She ought to be used to this but somehow it seemed worse as events moved toward an inevitable conclusion – good or bad.

"Easy there," Zach smoothly interrupted. He'd been quiet since they'd arrived at the airport but now his hand was on her elbow as if to reassure her tumultuous emotions. "This is not the time to lose control of the situation. We're almost on the plane."

"We're not going to argue." West placed his arm around her shoulders. Warm and reassuring, she breathed a hell of a lot easier when he was close. "Let's get through security and get out of this town."

Never having had the opportunity to fly before, Gigi was a newcomer to the joys of airport security. She panicked for a moment when a security agent separated her from Zach and West, the men headed for a conveyor belt at the end while she stayed in the middle. Her gaze kept searching them out, which was how frustrated an agent by not taking off her shoes and placing her handbag in a bin so it could be run through the x-ray machine. By the time she made it through her nerves were frazzled and she was gritting her teeth to keep from barking at anyone in a government uniform.

She shoved the too loose tennis shoes back on her feet, angrily tying the laces only to look up at West's frowning expression.

"You look pissed. Did they give you a pat down or something?"

"I didn't want to be separated from you."

West knelt down and brushed her trembling fingers from the laces, carefully tying them himself. "You're not mad, you're scared. But believe me, I never lost sight of you. Trust me, remember?"

West loved to be right but the gentle smile on his face was far from triumphant. He simply looked concerned as he patted her toes through the canvas sneaker.

"I do," Gigi sighed. "I'm...tense."

"I know, babe. Just stick with us a little while longer."

The way West had stood by her through all this crap? She was determined to stick with him until he didn't want her anymore. She didn't know when that would be but it was inevitable. He'd eventually want someone who wasn't trouble all the time, someone who knew how to be in a relationship.

"I'm so damn proud of you." Zach sat down next to her on the bench and lightly kissed her cheek. "You've been so brave through all of this. I wish I had been around to help you but you've taken care of yourself far better than most women would have in the same circumstances. You're my hero, Sis."

Laying her head on his shoulder, Gigi gave him a lopsided smile. "Thank you. I didn't realize how much I needed to hear that until now. I wish you had been there too. And Aubrey, of course."

West glanced at his watch and grimaced. "We need to get a move on. The plane is probably already boarding. We might actually pull this off."

Without a hitch. Within fifteen minutes the three of them were sitting in their seats – first class, courtesy of West – and winging their way over the heartland of America. For the first time that morning Gigi's heart rate and breathing were normal.

How long would they stay that way?

Chapter Twenty-One

WITH A WEARY sigh West tossed his small suitcase on the bed in the hotel room located on the outskirts of downtown Chicago. Large and bright, the room connected to a replica next door where Zach would sleep. Decorated in muted shades of green, the rooms boasted a king-sized bed, a small table with two chairs, a dresser, and a large bathroom with both a shower and a jetted tub. He'd have to thank Travis for the recommendation.

The connecting door was currently open so that Gigi and Zach could move back and forth freely between the rooms. The siblings has spent the flight sharing stories of their life since they'd been separated and West had tried to give them the space they needed to bond again. Already Zach was extremely protective of his little sister, an excellent trait as far as West was concerned.

"Do you mind?" West indicated the connecting door. "I need to make a call and I don't want to bother you."

Gigi wrinkled her nose and settled into a chair in Zach's room. "You mean you don't want us bothering you with our chatter. Go ahead and close it."

West glanced at Zach and the man nodded in agreement. "It's okay. I used the deadbolt. We're good."

Sliding the door closed, West pulled his phone from his pocket, using his thumb to press the buttons. Jared had left a message a few hours ago and West was anxious to find out the latest news.

Pressing the phone to his ear, he peered out the large picture window that gave him a spectacular view of the Chicago skyline. Jared picked up on the second ring.

"Are you there?"

West chuckled at Jared's abrupt greeting. The former sheriff was certainly a man of few words.

"We're here in Chicago," West agreed. "We just checked into the hotel. I already have a message from Wyatt that he and Shiloh are fine. They lost the tail Morton put on them when they turned north. How are things there? How's Shane?"

"Improving to the point he's grouchier than hell. He should get out of the hospital in the morning and it's not a moment too soon. The nurses were about to take up a petition to have him transferred to another hospital."

"And the authorities? Where do we stand with them?"

"Cleared. The video at the gas station shows that we were ambushed although it looked like the local prosecutor might want to make a name for himself using the case. But your brother's contacts squashed that pretty quickly."

"Jason knows a few people," West chuckled, his gaze swinging back to the connecting door. He could hear the soft murmur of voices but nothing out of the ordinary.

"It wasn't Jason that fixed things, although I'm sure he could have. It was your older brother Travis. He must have friends in high places is all I can say."

West shouldn't have been surprised. Travis traveled in the rarified air of big business. Cutthroat and dog eat dog, West hadn't thought those with a view from the top went out of their way to help someone out.

Unless they wanted something.

"I'm glad to hear it. Did he get on the plane okay?"

"He did. He should be there in the next few hours." West heard the shuffling of papers in the background. "Listen, I have some news on Gigi's sister Aubrey."

West's stomach tightened at Jared's tone. "You said that like it's a bad thing. Talk to me."

"I found a few things. She'd been adopted into a family so her last name changed to Grayson. That's why Gigi couldn't find her. Aubrey is a personal assistant during the day and attends night school twice a week working on a business degree. Not married. No kids. No major debt. No arrest record. Not even a speeding ticket. According to her neighbors she works hard and doesn't make too much noise."

None of that sounded scary which made West worry even more.

"She sounds like a model citizen. What haven't you told me?"

There was a heavy sigh on the other end of the line. "Her employer is Alan Morton."

West's fingers gripped the phone and he swore under his breath. "That son of a bitch. I wonder how long he's known her and Zach's whereabouts. Did he know when Gigi was with him and he kept them a secret? Now we know how they found us in Vegas. They knew we'd go see Zach."

It wasn't professional but West have a deep hankering to punch Alan Morton right in the gut. Or the jaw.

"That's a good question but I'm more worried about you, Zach, and Gigi. Aubrey is his ace in the hole, so to speak. He knows Gigi wants to reunite their family and I'm guessing he'll use the sister as a pawn."

An expendable one. If there was one thing Morton had proven it was that his obsession was with Gigi and only Gigi. Unlike many stalkers he hadn't transferred his so-called affections to another woman in the last two years. Once Aubrey was of no use to Morton he'd probably get rid of her in a most ruthless fashion.

"Jesus, I hate this guy. Now I have to worry about the safety of not only Gigi and her brother but her sister too. I'm glad Travis will be here soon. Did Jason say when that agent was going to contact us?"

"Soon. Maybe even today. By the way, his name is Faulkner. Jason says he's a good man."

West's brother wasn't the biggest fan of many of the agents he'd worked with through the years so that was high praise.

"Can you send me Aubrey's contact information? Once we put Morton behind bars Gigi is going to want to see her right away."

"Will do. I'll keep digging into Morton's background. Maybe we can find a smoking gun to help the government's case. From what Jason said they have a paper trail but nothing directly tied to him."

West chuckled, remembering a few past cases. "Juries these days want more than circumstantial evidence. They want a confession or forensics. Documents don't excite them the way fingerprints do."

"I know that all too well," Jared laughed. "I'd better let you go. I'll call you with any news."

West disconnected and shoved the phone back in his pocket. Staring at the closed connecting door, the unfamiliar feeling of indecision kept him from joining Zach and Gigi. He hated the feeling, not knowing what to do or say. If he told Gigi that they'd found her sister she'd want to see her right away. Today if she could.

But Aubrey worked for Morton... That brought up all sorts of scenarios that West didn't even want to contemplate. One was that Morton would use Aubrey as bait. The second was that she would be brainwashed by Morton into hurting Gigi.

Was Aubrey Grayson part of Alan Morton's criminal organization?

✦　✦　✦

"HE LOVES YOU. Anyone can see it."

Gigi and Zach were sitting in his room, him on the bed and her in a chair, while West caught up on his calls. It was still hard to believe that her brother was back in her life after all this time but here he was, full of brotherly concern and advice. He'd somehow managed to get her to admit she was in love with West but that she didn't think he'd stay with her in the long run.

"I believe that he loves me." West wouldn't have said it if it wasn't true. "But that doesn't mean that I have what it takes to make him happy. I don't know a darn thing about marriage or kids or even what a happy family life is supposed to look like. Eventually he's going to figure that out and he'll get tired of it. He'll want someone who doesn't have my problems."

Zach scowled and leaned forward his hands on his knees. "Once we get Morton behind bars you won't have any more problems. No serious ones, anyway."

Gigi ran her finger down the side of the plastic water bottle, the condensation dripping onto the table. "That will only reveal my shortcomings. Right now he's focused on getting Alan but eventually it will be just me and him. He'll see…all my flaws."

She didn't mind being imperfect. Everyone was. But the things that marred who she was were the exact things West would want in a life partner. She was clueless as to how to be in love.

"That's bullshit," Zach snorted. "You can learn how to be in a relationship and as for family, well, I love you and always have. You say the same. I bet Aubrey does too. Shit, after all these years and all we've been through if that isn't love then I don't know what is. You never gave up, Sis. I'm thinking you could give other people lessons on what being a family really means."

She wanted to believe.

"Mom didn't love us," she said, her voice dropping almost to a whisper. It hurt to even say it out loud but it was the truth. "If your own mother can't love you what hope do you have of inspiring it in someone else?"

Zach's lips flattened into a grim line and his eyes narrowed. "Mom couldn't love us because she spent most of her time at the bottom of a bottle. She had a sickness. A disease. She was so wrapped up in it she couldn't see straight. But on those few occasions she was sober she did try. I think she loved us as much as she was capable. Was it enough? Clearly not, but I've moved past it and you need to also. Don't let the past dictate your future. West loves you and you love him. Don't make this more complicated than it is."

Gigi pondered his words as she stared sightlessly at the ceiling. "Have you ever loved someone? Did they love you back?"

His hard expression immediately softened and he nodded with a smile. "Yes, I have known love. It wasn't especially kind to me. It didn't work out but I don't regret it. She was a sweet girl."

She reached across the space and laced her fingers with his. "What happened?"

"The war." Zach shrugged as if it didn't matter anymore. "We had both just graduated from high school and I didn't have two nickels to rub together. My adopted family was wonderful but they weren't loaded or anything. I enlisted and was sent overseas. She went to college. We tried to write but you know how that goes. Long distance relationships are hard, and even harder when you're barely an adult. She's probably married with three kids by now. I hope she's happy. She deserved it."

"That's very generous of you." Gigi was bowled over by the magnanimous sentiments. "I don't think I'd be as wonderful if West moved on. I'd be very unhappy."

Zach tilted his head and studied her face. "I was sad. But that's okay. Life is sad sometimes. Just because she and I didn't work out doesn't mean that what we had was a failure. She and my adopted parents taught me something really important."

"What?"

"That I was worthy of love. I think you might have skipped over that lesson somewhere. You're good enough for West to love you. I think all this stuff about you not knowing how to have a family is a smokescreen for what really ails you. You don't think you deserve him."

Looking down at the carpet, Gigi plucked at the fabric of her shirt. "Did you study to be a psychologist when you were in the Middle East?"

Zach laughed and levered to his feet. "Nope. I'm not smart enough. But I can see when a person is in great pain and Gigi, you are hurting all over. Between Mom and this Morton asshole you're confused about a few things, but I swear to you right now that West Anderson is one lucky son of a bitch to have you love him. If he doesn't treat you right I'll put a steel-toed boot so far up his ass he'll be walking funny from here to Easter."

The picture of Zach kicking West's ass made her smile and giggle. "I'm glad you're my brother."

He took her hands and pulled her to her feet. "I'm glad you're my sister. Why don't we go see if West has any news? We're in Chicago and that means we're close to finding Aubrey."

If Alan didn't find them first.

If he knew they were in Chicago it wouldn't be long before he came after Gigi. The clock was ticking.

Chapter Twenty-Two

S TANDING IN THE bathroom of his hotel room West taped the wires to Travis's chest, wincing at the thought of pulling all of it off later tonight. Travis had shaved his chest so that was in his favor, but it was still going to hurt like a son of a bitch.

"You don't have to do this. We can wait for Agent Faulkner to get what we need and then arrest Morton. I talked to him right before you arrived and he's working on it. He's trying to get an arrest warrant. He has someone on the inside but he didn't say who."

Even as he said it West knew they couldn't hang around like sitting ducks waiting for Alan Morton to come get them. It was far better to be on the offensive in a situation like this. While dangerous, it was even more treacherous to sit tight and hope that nothing happened.

That was a losing proposition. Morton wanted Gigi and would do anything to get her. The fact that they'd been in Chicago less than a day and he hadn't tried anything yet worried West. The diversion of Wyatt and Shiloh wouldn't throw Morton off their scent permanently. The most they could hope for was a few hours of peace and that time had ticked away.

Travis nodded toward the door where Gigi and Zach sat on the other side relaxing after dinner. They'd ordered room service and tried to pretend that nothing special was happening tonight.

"Can she wait that long? She wants to see her sister and I don't blame her. Let's not make tonight into a bigger deal than it really is. I'm going in and see if I can talk to him. That's it. Maybe he'll say something and maybe he won't."

He was downplaying the very real danger of doing anything within Morton's sphere. From what Gigi had told them he had an army of paid flunkies to do the dirty work.

"I should be doing this," West muttered, frustration making his neck and shoulders tight. "This isn't your battle to fight."

Travis buttoned up his shirt and tucked it into his dark slacks. "You can't. We have to assume he knows who you are and has some sort of intel, even if it's only a picture and a short bio. No, it's better if I go. I doubt he knows or cares about me."

Travis was right but it didn't make this any easier.

"The rich gambler. That's your play tonight?"

A grin spreading across his face, Travis retrieved a blue silk tie from his suitcase. "The richest. I'll toss around hundreds like they're dollar bills and lose some money playing blackjack or poker. Maybe roulette. The idea is to get Morton's attention and then befriend him. I want to get him talking. Maybe I'll tell him I'm in the market for some female companionship tonight."

The idea of an Anderson man ever paying for sex was ludicrous but hopefully Travis wouldn't have too many lovely ladies hanging on his arm this evening. West's brother had no problem finding plenty of willing women wherever he went.

"What would your current girlfriend say about that?" West

teased. "I'd hate for this little mission to endanger any relationship you might have going."

Sitting on the bed, Travis strapped a gun around his ankle before pulling on his boot. "Adele and I parted ways a few weeks ago."

Adele had been an icy Nordic blonde that stood six feet tall in her stocking feet. Beautiful but aloof, she'd made a poor impression on West when they'd been introduced. Clearly she didn't like sharing Travis either with friends or family and hadn't bothered to hide that little factoid. In other words, she'd been a bitch the entire evening.

"What did you do this time?"

Travis grimaced and leaned forward resting his elbows on his knees. "She didn't like all the hours that I spend at work. Between my regular work schedule and the mayoral race I apparently took advantage of her good nature. She called me a selfish rat bastard when she walked out."

"How's that broken heart?"

"I may never recover." Travis smirked and then stood, straightening his tie. "I wish her well but she's definitely not someone I could take home to Mom and Dad."

"Was that the plan? Are you looking to settle down, big brother? You are on the wrong side of forty."

Despite being the oldest, Travis was the most adamant about avoiding commitment at all costs. The people of Tremont called West a womanizer but that was only because they didn't have any idea what Travis was up to when he was jetting around the world. He was ass deep in swooning females.

"Not in the foreseeable future. Maybe someday. Honestly,

there are simply too many beautiful women in this world to pick just one. I'm happy for you and Jason though."

Typical Travis.

"Maybe you need to change up the type of women you date."

Another smirk. "Why in the hell would I do that?"

"Anyone can see that you are a deeply unhappy man." West couldn't even say the words with a straight face, his shoulders shaking with laughter. "Morose. Depressed, even."

"I'll try to put on a happy face for the evening ahead. Are we ready?"

West nodded, slipping his jacket over his shoulder holster. Zach would stay here with Gigi while West accompanied Travis to Morton's club. He'd stay in the car listening to the recording and monitoring for trouble.

"Let me say goodbye to Gigi and we'll get out of here."

That all too familiar rush of adrenaline was coursing through West's veins. It felt good to have a plan of action. Hell, it felt good to be doing something instead of being in wait mode. He was damn tired of reacting to whatever Morton threw at them. It was time to put that bastard on the defensive.

"I'VE CALLED THREE times today. I don't like having to chase you down, Morton."

Alan held the phone away from his ear, not because his boss Caleb Deardon was speaking too loudly but because the tone was soft and dangerous. Deardon had shown himself to be someone to be reckoned with when he was pissed off. Several people had simply disappeared never to be heard from again when they crossed the man who had clawed his way up through the organization in record time. Alan didn't want to join the ranks of the missing but there were things that needed his attention today.

Georgette and her phalanx of devoted bodyguards was at the top of that list. It hadn't taken him long to realize they'd fooled his men in Vegas and flown to Chicago. It had taken even less time to find her hotel despite her companion paying with cash. A few calls to the cab companies plus a bribe or two and he'd found out all he needed to know. She was now in Chicago and he was getting impatient. Dammit, he'd waited two years for this.

Alan pressed the speaker button on the phone and set it down on the dark oak desk that was the centerpiece of his home office. Decorated in subdued earth tones by Georgette before she left, it was his favorite room in the house.

"I didn't get the messages until a few minutes ago, Caleb. I've been taking care of a few things today."

Alan kept his voice even, not letting his nerves get the best of him when speaking to Deardon even as a trickle of sweat ran down his temple. Caleb Deardon was one cold son of a bitch who would have sold his mother into prostitution if it made him a buck.

"And by *things* do you mean that woman?"

Stiffening in his chair, Alan didn't answer right away. Deardon had been in the organization when Georgette was in Chicago before but he hadn't then been in charge. The fact that he knew about Alan's personal life illustrated the reach and power he had.

OLIVIA JAYMES

Alan didn't like it at all.

If he knew about Georgette what else did he know? And who in Alan's organization was talking?

"I'm not sure what you mean."

Maybe Deardon was just fishing for information.

"I'm talking about Georgette Sidney. Is this going to be a problem, Morton? We don't need you doing anything that gets the attention of the police. Do you understand?"

Deardon knew her name. Not good.

"Of course, Caleb. I'd never do anything to jeopardize what we have going on. Georgette is back in Chicago and I'm sure I'll be seeing her soon, that's all."

"Willingly or unwillingly? I mean it. Don't do something stupid over a female. Jesus, they're a dime a dozen, Morton. If you want a woman I'll send one over. Name the height, weight, and hair color. She'll give you a night you'll never forget. But leave the ones that don't want you alone. It isn't worth the trouble."

There was no one like Georgette. That's why Alan had to have her back. No one else would do.

He wasn't going to fucking explain himself to Deardon. This could all be handled quietly with a minimum of fuss. She would come to Alan of her own free will. He'd made sure of that.

"You're worried over nothing. It's all going to be fine. I promise."

"It better fucking be fine because if you do anything that makes the cops start looking at us I'll make life very difficult for you. Mark my words. I'm coming by the club tonight to talk more about this so be there. No excuses."

Screw you, Deardon.

"I hear you and it will all be fine. You can rest assured."

The line was dead. Deardon had hung up, a fact Alan was most grateful for. Verbal sparring with Deardon over Georgette wouldn't end well. The man didn't understand. No one did, really. She belonged to Alan, and in the next twenty-four hours she'd be back where she belonged.

Chapter Twenty-Three

"ENJOY YOURSELF, MR. Armstrong. I think you'll find we offer any sort of entertainment you might require."

The nightclub's manager gave a small nod and turned on his heel to stride away, leaving Travis alone just inside the entrance to the secret illegal gambling room in Morton's nightclub. It had been almost too easy for him to gain access. At first he'd stayed in the nightclub area flashing large amounts of cash and tipping wildly. Cozying up to a cute cocktail waitress, he'd brought up the subject of gambling on the premises and she'd hooked him up with the manager. After generously oiling that palm he'd been escorted upstairs. Clearly Morton's men were motivated by cash which was a fortunate thing.

Travis's back and neck were still damp with sweat, his heart still beating too fast from waiting to gain access to the VIP room as it was called. If the manager guy hadn't bought into his cover bad things could have happened. West had warned Travis about undercover cops beaten up and even shot if the suspect didn't completely believe in the persona. It had been a relief when the sound of slot machines and roulette wheels had been heard through the closed door.

"I'm in," he said quietly. There was no two-way communication between himself and West. His brother could hear what was going on and that was it. Currently West sat in a rental car across the street listening in case there was any trouble. Travis had assured his brother that he could handle himself so intervention would be unnecessary, but West's adage when it came to surveillance work had always been better safe than sorry.

"What can I get you, sir?"

A busty blonde waitress in a tight dress smiled invitingly at Travis.

"Jameson on the rocks."

She leaned forward slightly, giving him a much better view of her double D's.

"Anything else?"

Her tone was complete seduction and not a bit coy. It was all out there in the open. She was ready to play with a man who had a big…bank account.

"Just the drink, thank you."

Normally Travis might not mind some company but this evening wasn't about pleasure. This was work and getting Morton out of Gigi's life. After everything that girl had been through she deserved some happiness. From the way she and West were looking at each other it appeared they'd found it together.

Travis was happy for his brother but that didn't mean he wanted to find a woman and settle down himself. That was the problem with happy couples. They wanted everyone to be happy and to them that meant in a relationship. Travis was pretty damn estatic being single. He was never alone unless he wanted to be.

The waitress brought him the drink and he murmured his thanks while sliding a twenty into a small pocket on her dress. She gave him a dazzling smile and leaned forward, her strong perfume cloying in the enclosed space.

"Let me know if you need anything else. My name is Lisa."

Sipping his whiskey, Travis's gaze settled on Alan Morton standing next to the roulette wheel, a stunning brunette to his right. Dressed in a deceptively simple midnight blue cocktail dress, the woman was beautiful enough to be a model or a Hollywood actress. Average height but not skinny, the strapless satin skimmed her generous curves and pushed up a pair of obviously real breasts that begged to be worshipped. Sable colored hair with golden highlights was swept off her graceful neck and secured with a gold barrette. From this distance it didn't appear that she was wearing a face full of makeup, her cheeks flushed and her skin glowing with life. Naturally beautiful?

He needed to see her up close and personal.

Travis took a step forward but then hesitated. In an instant he'd gone from being all business to lusting after a woman he'd seen across a crowded room. It was cliché and also stupid. He needed to keep his head in the game if he didn't want to end up dead. Alan Morton wasn't a man to take lightly. He was making too much of a female. In all probability she was no different than every other woman Travis had met. Lovely to look at but far too interested in his money.

Taking a deep breath, he strode up to the roulette table, keeping his shoulders relaxed but making sure his posture and bearing spoke of confidence. He'd learned that trick when attending Harvard. Travis had been the nouveau riche kid there, brought up around cows and pickup trucks. He hadn't immediately fit in and had been fascinated by how self-assured those around him seemed. It was as if they had no doubts about, well, anything. He'd quickly learned to emulate their sanguine attitude while at the same time exuding an alpha vibe that came in quite handy during business negotiations. It had held him in good stead all these years and he called upon every little trick he knew tonight to get under Morton's skin and get him to talk.

Stepping to the right of Morton, Travis placed a few chips on red nineteen, completely ignoring anyone around him. Rich and powerful people liked to be noticed and nothing snagged their attention faster than when they were overlooked.

The wheel spun and landed on a black twenty-eight. The dealer deftly swept the losing chips on the table away. Travis placed more chips down on red nineteen while keeping his focus on the wheel and not the man standing to his left. The wheel spun again and the numbers blurred before his eyes. If he kept silent it should prod–.

"Does the number nineteen have significance for you? If not, you should play either red or black. Your odds of winning are higher."

Bingo.

Travis gave Morton the barest of glances before dismissing him with a nod. "It does."

This time red thirty came up and Travis's chips were once again swept away. He sipped his whiskey before placing two more chips down on red nineteen. Again.

"You seem very determined with that bet. Let me introduce myself. I'm Alan Morton. I own this club."

Travis transferred the glass of scotch to his left hand before turning toward Morton and holding out his right. A few inches shorter, Alan Morton looked to be in his late thirties although Travis sucked at guessing ages. Boyishly handsome at one time from the pictures in the file, Morton now had the beginnings of sagging jowls and neck plus a little extra around the middle. He didn't look like a criminal mastermind but more like a used car salesman with his dark hair parted on the side.

Of course no car salesman would be able to afford that suit. It appeared to be bespoke dark navy blue. Probably Italian.

"Travis Armstrong." He shook Morton's hand and looked around the club appreciatively. "Nice place you got here. It's all yours?"

"I have a partner," Morton answered casually. "I don't think I've seen you in here before. Who referred you?"

So that's what this was about. Morton wanted to know how Travis had found out about the gambling room. Suspicious, wasn't he? In his profession that was probably a wise thing.

"Sheldon. But it's been quite awhile since I've seen him. I'm always traveling. Haven't been in Chicago in several years, but then it never seems to change."

Travis had pulled the name of the richest, most powerful man he knew in Chicago out of his ass and he hoped like hell it would work. It was his own fault he wasn't prepared for a question he should have anticipated.

"Milo Sheldon?" Morton smiled and nodded. "He hasn't been here for months. He's been spending a lot of time in Palm

Springs since the divorce."

"Shame about him and Karen," Travis said, breathing a little easier. Morton had bought the bullshit. "I thought they seemed happy."

"Things aren't always as they seem, Mr. Armstrong."

No shit. Alan Morton appeared to be completely normal. Travis could see how Gigi was taken in.

"Sadly, that's true," Travis agreed. "Are you married?"

"Engaged. And yourself?"

Was the asshole talking about Gigi? If so, he really was batcrap crazy. And from the stiffening of Morton's shoulders he didn't like being asked personal questions.

Too damn bad.

Travis let his gaze wander around the room, resting on the stunning brunette he'd noticed earlier. "Too many beautiful women to limit myself."

Morton smiled when he saw where Travis was looking. "Someday you'll meet a woman that will change you, Mr. Armstrong. You'll do anything, even move heaven and earth just so she's safe and happy. Everything I do is for her."

"Everything I do is for me. I like money. And power. But then I didn't have any of that growing up. It means more to you if you're not born with it."

Morton nodded in agreement. "I find the most motivated men to be those that were not born with wealth."

"You appear to be a self-made man," Travis challenged. "I too admire those that can pull themselves up by their bootstraps. You have a popular nightclub in the heart of the city. But a smart man like you? I bet you've diversified. I'm in cattle, oil, and mining. If one is down something else is up."

Morton's eyes narrowed and his smile flickered. "I've got a few irons in the fire here and there."

"More than a few, I'm betting."

Morton stroked his chin, still smiling although it didn't reach his dark, cold eyes. "I never bet, Mr. Henderson. It was good to meet you but my manager is signaling me. If you need anything this evening don't hesitate to ask. We're here to serve."

With that Alan Morton strode toward the entrance while Travis inwardly cursed. He hadn't been able to get anything out of the guy who was clearly beyond paranoid. But then if the Feds were investigating Travis, he would be overly suspicious too.

Eyeing the patrons at the bar, Travis hoped at least one of them was a regular here. If Morton wouldn't talk then perhaps someone would speak *about* him.

Time for Plan B.

✦   ✦   ✦

"HE'S THERE." WEST lowered the volume on Travis's conversation with some drunk in the nightclub so he could hear Jason's friend Agent Faulkner more clearly on his cell. "Travis is in there right now wearing a wire. He's hoping to get some information to help your case."

"Shit," Faulkner hissed. Despite the lousy connection, his expletive came through loud and clear. "Didn't your brother Jason call you and let you know that I was planning a raid tonight? I've got the club surrounded by a dozen agents plus SWAT. Fuck. I don't want your brother caught in any crossfire."

It wasn't like West's detail-oriented brother not to call about something this important, but there had to be some reasonable explanation.

"When did you talk to Jason?"

A small silence. "I didn't actually talk to him. I left a message on his phone about two hours ago when I knew the mission was for sure."

"That explains it. Shane got out of the hospital this afternoon and they're transporting him back to Tremont. They may be on the road where the service is spotty or even still in the air."

Shane's father flew a small private plane and it would make sense for him to fly Shane home instead of subjecting him to a long car ride or a commercial airline. Jason probably flew with them while Jared went back to Seattle to be with his wife and baby. West had decided he didn't need the extra manpower in Chicago. Zach was working out well. Better than well actually. The man knew what he was doing when it came to personal security.

"Is there any way you can get your brother out of there? Can you call him?"

"I'll call him now. How much time does he have?"

"Five minutes."

Faulkner hung up abruptly and West didn't hesitate. Punching a few buttons, Travis's phone rang.

And rang.

And rang.

Son of a bitch. Why wasn't he picking up?

West could hear his brother speaking on the recording sounding perfectly normal and relaxed.

He hit the end button before quickly typing out a text and

pressing send.

Sucking in a breath West watched the front doors of the club, waiting for his brother to come out. With each passing second his nerves stretched thin, causing sweat to trickle down his neck and back.

West's fingers fumbled with his cell again, trying to call Travis one more time even as the clock ticked down. A SWAT team was about to raid the club and no one would be safe.

No answer. Shit.

One glance at his watch told West that time was up. Even from this distance West could see the dark shadows of officers rushing through the front doors. West's guts twisted into a knot as the sound of gunfire pierced the dark night along with flashes of light through the windows.

Upstairs, where the gambling room was located.

Travis was in the middle of a firefight.

And there wasn't a damn thing West could do about it.

Chapter Twenty-Four

"THEY'VE BEEN GONE for hours. Maybe I should call West."

Gigi paced the hotel room, her hands wrung together in worry. West and Travis had gone to Alan's club despite her pleading to the contrary. They wanted to learn as much as they could and see if perhaps they might get some information that might help the government's case. They'd known it was a long shot but sitting around in a hotel room waiting for the Feds wasn't something these Anderson men did well.

Zach was sitting at the small table in her room, half watching television and half watching her. "You're going to wear a hole in the carpet. Just relax. I haven't known West Anderson all that long but I got the distinct impression that he can handle himself in just about any situation. His brother didn't look any less capable. How about we check out the mini-bar?"

"That's not a bad idea but I'm not sure I can eat when I'm this nervous."

Her heart was racing faster with each passing moment. At this rate she was going to stroke out before West and Travis came back.

Zach chuckled and pulled open the door of the mini-bar.

"Who said anything about eating? I was talking about busting open some booze. We've got Coke. I bet there's some rum down here." He held up two small bottles in triumph. "Rum and vodka. There's gin in here too."

Gigi reached for her glass on the dresser and slapped it down on the table. "That sounds like a plan. I swear West Anderson does this on purpose to make me crazy."

Zach poured her a rum and Coke, generous on the alcohol. "Drink this and calm down. I'm sure everything is fine."

She took a big gulp enjoying the burn all the way to her now empty stomach. She'd been too nervous to eat dinner so it wasn't going to take much rum to make her tipsy.

"I just wish he'd call–"

She didn't get to finish her sentence. The door of the hotel room flew open to reveal West and Travis – alive and in one piece – although the older brother looked a trifle worse for wear. There was a small cut over one eye and his impeccably tailored suit had a few dark spots on it that hadn't been there when he left.

"Are you alright?" Gigi raced to West's side and wrapped her arms around his middle, breathing in his familiar scent. He patted her on the back and pressed a quick, reassuring kiss to her lips.

"We're fine. Agent Faulkner's men raided the club and Travis was still in there."

Alarmed, Gigi's gaze jerked back to Travis running up and down his form, but her original inspection proved correct. Other than a cut he appeared to be okay.

"I'm fine. Really."

Travis held up his hands in a sign of surrender as Zach stepped forward to give the oldest Anderson brother the once over.

"I'll get the first aid kit. Then I'll make you both a drink. I think you could use it." Zach pointed to the still oozing gash on Travis's forehead. "How'd that happen?"

"A drink is exactly what we need." Travis fell into a chair and groaned. "When the SWAT team raided the place there were a few people who didn't want to surrender. Gunshots were fired and I pushed a woman at the bar to the floor to protect her. She fought me for a few moments until she realized what I was trying to do. She was wearing jewelry and it cut me. It's not a big deal."

Zach dabbed at the injury with a cotton ball soaked in antiseptic, making Travis wince and curse. "Shit, that hurts worse than actually getting hit. Give me that."

Gigi had to suppress her laughter as Travis snatched the cotton from Zach's fingers, a scowl on his face.

West tilted her chin up so she was looking him in the eyes. "They got him. He was arrested and now he's in jail. We watched him being marched out and placed in a police car."

Her breath whooshed out of her body and she sagged in relief against West. The fluttering of a million butterfly wings could be felt in her abdomen as it began to dawn on her what this truly meant.

Freedom.

Free to come and go wherever and whenever she pleased. Freedom to live her life without Alan's control. Free to love and be loved.

Free to have a future with West.

Overwhelmed and in shock, she had to sit on the bed as her knees gave out and her entire body shook. West settled next to her, his arm around her shoulders reassuring her that she hadn't imagined this. It wasn't a dream. This was real and it was happening to her after all this time. Her running and hiding days were over.

"Easy, babe. Just relax. This is a good thing."

Logically, she knew that but at the moment emotion had taken control. Tears began to leak out of her eyes and down her cheeks as the news began to sink into her brain. She hadn't realized how on edge her nerves had been, how deep the fear had wormed its way into her very soul.

She'd been like this for two long years, longer really once she added in the time with Alan. It had become her *normal* and now it was gone. For a second as she'd felt the layers of protection she'd built up slip away, she'd scrambled to pull them around her again, not sure what or who she was if she wasn't this…a woman frightened and on the run.

His callused fingers brushed the tears away as he pulled her into his strong, warm embrace, his lips capturing hers in an all too brief kiss. The emotion that was spilling over was indeed gratitude but it was so much more than that.

It was love. She loved West. Deeply. Irrevocably.

This was no crush or friendship love. This was real. The kind that lasted forever and made you want to share everything with someone, even the bad times.

Holy crap on a cracker. It scared the hell out of her.

It didn't matter that she didn't know anything about love or family. If she couldn't have West Anderson in her life it wouldn't be the same.

"It is amazing. I'm just trying to process it all. I didn't expect you to walk in and tell me it was all over."

She congratulated herself for getting the words past the lump that had formed in her throat. She simply didn't have the capacity at this juncture to express her feelings.

"I didn't think it would all happen tonight but it did. I don't know why they changed their minds and raided the club tonight but it's a done deal. It's time to stop looking over your shoulder and start looking ahead. With me."

A quick glance up and she could see Zach and Travis sneaking into the connecting room, sliding the door closed after them, leaving Gigi and West alone.

She gazed up into his soft green eyes, so full of love it made her heart ache. She'd finally done something right. The day she'd said yes to West's request for a date was the day she'd taken the first step to putting her life back on track.

"With you," she echoed, the words coming out choked but audible. "I love you."

West's smile widened, that dimple she loved so much making an appearance. "I love you too, babe. More than you can imagine. Everything is going to be okay from now on. I promise you."

He'd shown her every single day that she'd known him – when West Anderson made a promise, he kept it.

"I know it will. You take good care of me, handsome."

West lowered himself to the bed and lounged back on the pillows, his hands under his head and a grin on his face. "All part of the service I offer."

Gigi climbed onto the bed and crawled over to West, her legs on either side of his muscular thighs.

"Is there any way I can thank you, Detective Anderson?"

"I'm sure there are a few ways," he smirked, clearly trying not to laugh out loud. It shouldn't be this hot in the hotel room but suddenly Gigi was overheated. "Did you have something in mind?"

She did. Nudity and sweat were involved.

Leaning down, she pressed her lips to his collarbone and his warm, masculine smell filled her nostrils. It wrapped around her, inching up her arousal even as he placed his hands on her cheeks and lifted her face so he could capture her mouth with his in a long, drugging kiss.

West grasped the bottom of her t-shirt and tugged it over her head before reaching behind her and squeezing the hooks of her bra. Cool air puckered her nipples and sent shivers down her spine as he discarded her clothing into a heap on the floor. His fingers worked their way under the elastic waistband of her yoga pants and he had them sliding down her legs within seconds, his rough touch on her skin turning her knees to jelly. Her panties followed the same path until she was completely naked to his gaze and touch.

His hands cupped her breasts while this thumbs brushed the tips until she ached with need. "I think you like that, babe. Do you want me to stop?"

His tone was dark and playful at the same time and her heart tripped in her chest at the promise of fun and pleasure in his words.

"Don't you dare," she choked out, swallowing hard to dislodge the lump that had taken up residence in her throat as he kissed and caressed her more than willing body. "Fuck me."

"I'm planning on that. But I think I'd like to play a little bit first."

Liquid heat was already flying through her veins and a bar of arousal had formed in her abdomen but when West was in this mood… there was no hurrying him along. She bit her lip as he flicked his tongue around a pebbled nipple, drawing a ragged moan from her lips. The ridge of his erection pressed against her sex and she ground herself against him showing him in no uncertain terms exactly what she needed and wanted.

Chuckling, West simply wrapped his fingers around her wrists and placed them behind her back.

"So naughty. I think you might need a spanking before we're done here tonight. But first you're going to be a good girl and keep your hands exactly where I've placed them while I have some fun. No breaking the rules or I'll make you wait for your pleasure."

He'd do just that too.

"Sadist," she hissed but obeyed, keeping her hands pinned to her lower back while his fingers skimmed up her ribs and began to tweak at her nipples until she was squirming and writhing on top of his denim covered length. The friction against her clit only served to send her arousal higher, flames dancing on her sensitive flesh.

"If you hated it you would be kicking me in the balls. I think you like this more than you want to admit. Now scoot up here and stay still."

Kicking him in the balls wasn't off the list. Yet. But if he was planning to do what she thought he was going to do she'd mark it off permanently.

Still on her knees and straddling West, she crawled farther up his body until her slit was right above his mouth. Grasping her hips, he positioned her exactly as he wanted right before running his tongue up and down her folds until she let out a half scream-half moan. Her toes curled and her head fell back as pleasure washed over her like the incoming tide.

"Might want to keep it down," West chuckled, his voice muffled. "Your dearest brother is in the next room."

With his tongue dancing over her swollen clit she couldn't form the words to make a retort. Instead she groaned and squirmed in response but he only clamped his fingers on her hips more tightly, holding her in place as his tongue drove her slowly out of her ever loving mind. Each flick sent her closer and closer to the edge until he had her shaking with an arousal so powerful it was almost painful.

"Now," she pleaded, her tongue snaking out to wet her dry lips as beads of sweat trickled down the valley between her breasts. She was on fire from the inside out, flames consuming every inch of her skin. "Fuck me now."

The breath was knocked out of her as he rolled her under him, his fingers tearing at his button-fly. Cursing, he shoved his jeans downs his legs and she reached for him impatiently. Hard and ready, he pulsed under her eager fingers and she caressed the velvety flesh stretched over solid steel.

"Are you ready for me, babe?"

Gigi slid her legs apart, her feet braced on the mattress as West positioned himself between her thighs. He thrust home in one mighty stroke and she cried out at the pleasure of being so deliciously filled. Her channel walls stretched to accommodate him but he didn't give her much opportunity to recover. Pulling out almost all the way, he thrust back in again and again, each stroke rubbing her clit so she was teetering on the precipice.

Digging her nails into his shoulder blades, she panted with each mind-bending stroke until she finally exploded in a flash of light. She bucked underneath him as pleasure poured through every vein and bone, sending her higher into the clouds than she'd ever been.

When West reached his own peak he groaned her name as his muscles tensed and bunched under her palms. She watched in rapt attention as he closed his gorgeous green eyes for only a moment before burying his face in her neck.

Her hands glided down his back, the flesh slick with sweat, to rest at the base of his spine. Cradling him in her arms, she pressed baby kisses on his chest and jaw, anywhere she could reach until he rolled over on his back, taking her with him. They lay that way, arms and legs entwined, as their breathing returned to normal.

It was at that moment it hit her.

She had her life back. That meant no more excuses, no more putting off all the things she wanted to do and see. The future was lying right beside her.

Chapter Twenty-Five

G IGI EXITED THE hotel the next morning with a sunny smile on her lips, her heart practically dancing the foxtrot in her chest. Today was the first day of her new life and nothing was going to stop her from living it to the fullest. Still breathless from her unlimited possibilities, she could barely contain the joy bubbling up inside. She had a future with the man she loved. True, she didn't know what that future entailed. Life didn't come with guarantees but now she had something to look forward to. Something to hope for.

West was back in the hotel room still asleep as they'd stayed up late, too excited to rest. There was a coffee shop just half a block down and she wanted to surprise him by picking up coffee and muffins for the two of them. It wasn't a fancy breakfast in bed but it was a start in showing him how much she loved him. She had a powerful urge to spoil the heck out of him.

A long black limousine with dark tinted windows pulled smoothly up to the curb and stopped, the back door opening. Gigi only barely registered its presence until Alan appeared from its depths, a smile on his face.

She stumbled and then froze, too frightened to move or even

breathe. She had to force herself to exhale as he stood there on the sidewalk, his intense gaze eating her up with his eyes. There was a look of triumph too in his expression. She'd seen it before when she would bend to his will, but nothing like this. His cheeks were ruddy with excitement and his entire body was coiled with tension as if he was holding himself back by sheer force of will.

"Georgette, I'm so glad to see you this morning."

Licking her suddenly dry lips, she tried to stay steady on suddenly shaky legs. "Alan…"

Her voice trailed off and she had to suck air into her aching lungs. Her voice was screaming inside her head to run, find West. Anyone. Just get away, but utter shock had frozen her limbs.

"I have a surprise for you, Georgette. One you're going to love. I've found your sister Aubrey. I know you've been looking for her. Don't you want to meet her? Reunite?"

That superior tone she knew only too well set her teeth on edge.

"I don't believe you," she whispered so softly she wasn't sure he could even hear her on this loud and busy city street, but he must have. Alan smiled and pointed inside the back of the limousine.

"I thought you might not so I brought proof. Aubrey, come say hello to your big sister."

Finally gathering control of her wits, Gigi was poised to flee when a young woman stuck her head out of the vehicle. A heart-shaped face with thick dark hair and eyes.

Aubrey. Grown, but Gigi would know her sister anywhere.

Shit. Shit. Shit.

Her sister's lips were trembling with fear and Gigi could no more run and leave her to the tender mercies of Alan than a small puppy or an infant. It was Gigi's fault that Aubrey was caught up in this in the first place.

"What do you want from me, Alan? You need to let Aubrey go."

Gigi congratulated herself at how strong and determined she sounded even when she was terrified inside. Alan stroked Aubrey's cheek, causing the young woman to shudder and press her lips together as if to smother a scream.

"I want you to get in and take a little ride with us. Of your own free will, of course. You know I'd never do anything to force you, Georgette."

God, she hated being called by her full name. Alan knew it too, which was why he did it. He'd always said he wanted to call her by a name no one else used. It had been his way of being so damn special.

Asshole.

"Let her go, Alan. This is between you and me," Gigi said between gritted teeth, her entire body shaking with a combination of fear and rage. He'd gone too far this time, using Aubrey against her.

"It was," he agreed. "Until you left. Now get in the car like a good girl. This just shows me that you can't be trusted to take care of yourself. You need me. You've always needed me."

A single tear was sliding down Aubrey's cheek. There wasn't anything left to do but admit that – for now – Alan had the upper hand.

Forgive me, West. I can't let him hurt my sister.

Steeling herself for what was to come, she stepped toward the curb but stopped in surprise when Alan's reached for her handbag.

"Your cell phone."

He had his hand out, waiting not so patiently. She reached in, wishing there was a gun in her purse instead of a billfold and a hairbrush and pulled out her cell, placing it on his outstretched palm. His fingers closed over it and then before she could protest he flung it against the brick building. The phone broke into pieces and rained down on the sidewalk while Alan watched with a cool smile on his face.

"Now we're ready to go. Have a seat, darling."

Tightening her grip on the strap of her purse she stepped into the limousine, the inside cool and dark. Two of Alan's minions, large and armed, sat on the opposite seat while Gigi slid next to Aubrey and grabbed her hand.

"It'll be okay," she said softly, squeezing Aubrey's cold fingers between her own. Gigi's palm was sticky with sweat but she was determined Alan wouldn't see her fear. Not anymore. She wouldn't give in this time. She'd fight to the very end.

Aubrey nodded but the fear was still there. Gig wrapped an arm around her sister, trying desperately to comfort the shaking young woman who clearly comprehended the gravity of the current situation. Alan was going to take them somewhere out of the way and keep them prisoner. With the cell phone smashed on the street she had no hope that West would be able to trace it, which she was sure was Alan's plan.

Gigi was on her own but this time was going to be different.

She'd learned to be strong and resourceful in the last two years. She'd learned to fight for her freedom and she didn't intend to stop now.

✦　　✦　　✦

WEST RE-READ THE note that Gigi had left on her pillow.

Gone to coffee shop. I'll be back with breakfast. Love you.

Smiling and feeling happier than he had in a long while, he levered up from the bed and reached for his blue jeans, tugging them up his legs. He wished she'd woken him before she left so he could go with her but he knew she was relishing her new-found freedom. She'd been scared and on the run for so long she had to be chomping at the bit to go somewhere – hell, any-where – all by herself.

Even if it was only a trip two doors down from the hotel.

He zipped up his jeans and grabbed a t-shirt from his suit-case, his mind already thinking about the day. They needed to contact Gigi's sister Aubrey who was probably upset that her boss was behind bars. He'd explain as much as he could and then hopefully she'd agree to travel back to Montana with them so she and Gigi could spend some time together. He wasn't as fond of big cities as Travis was, but if Aubrey wasn't willing to visit Tremont then he and Gigi would stay here in Chicago for a few weeks. Zach had said he was perfectly at ease doing either and that his employment situation was "casual", whatever that meant. West was pretty sure it meant that if Zach had to quit his job at the martial arts gym to spend time with his sisters he'd damn well do it.

West's cell on the bedside table chirped and he finished pulling the shirt over his head and reached for the phone.

Jared Monroe, Jason's computer research genius.

"You're calling early," West laughed, pressing the phone to his ear. "What time is it in Seattle?"

"Around six, but we live by the baby's schedule. I hope I didn't wake you up."

"I was awake. What's up? Is everything okay with Shane?"

West had received a text from his cousin last night that he was home and resting comfortably but that didn't mean he still didn't feel guilty about Shane's injuries. Hellfire, he was shot. West was going to have to buy Shane a car or something to make up for what happened.

"Everything is fine as far as I know. I talked to him last night and he sounded good. No, I'm calling about this Alan Morton guy. I've got some information you might find interesting. I just sent some photos to your email along with every detail I could find on your suspect. But you need to look at the pictures. You'll see what I mean."

"Talk to me," West said, flipping open the laptop and clicking on the email attachments. He didn't see much that interested him until he came across a picture of Morton's family when the man was a teenager. "Shit. Just…shit."

"That's what I said after I saw a picture of your girlfriend. They're dead ringers for each other, aren't they?"

West couldn't stop staring at the picture of the girl sitting next to a young Alan Morton, his brain having trouble comprehending what Jared was showing him. "Who is she?"

"Morton's stepsister, Anna. His father married her mother

when Morton was sixteen and Anna was fifteen. She died in a car crash three years later. There were two couples in the car and all of them had been drinking and partying. The driver lost control on a rainy night and hit a tree."

That's why Morton was so obsessed with Gigi. He wanted to replace Anna with a look alike. Sick bastard.

"That's why he never gave up."

"From what I've been able to find out from some of Morton's friends he was obsessed with his stepsister," Jared continued. "He never liked her boyfriends and he kept her on a tight leash – walking her to and from school and convincing his parents that she shouldn't be allowed to drive anywhere by herself. His friends thought that it was strange but he told them he felt protective because Anna was pretty wild and didn't always use the best judgment."

"That is fucked up about ten different ways."

"Apparently his attempt at controlling her only served to make her even more rebellious than your usual teenage girl. She drank, smoked, and basically ran around with the biggest losers in school. Of course that just made him more determined."

West sighed and closed the photo array. "I appreciate all the digging you've had to do to find this out. It explains a lot."

"Glad I could help. Let me know if there's anything else I can do."

West hung up but didn't even get to set his phone on the table before it was buzzing again. The name displayed read Agent Faulkner and West eagerly swiped the screen wanting to hear the latest news regarding Alan Morton.

"Anderson."

"This is Faulkner." The man sounded tired as if he'd been up all night. West wouldn't have been surprised. "I'm afraid I have some bad news."

West's heart sunk and his stomach churned as bile rose in his throat. "He's going to make bail today isn't he? The bastard."

"It's worse. You need to keep your girlfriend close to you. Morton's *already* made bail. He's got friends in high places in Chicago and he called in a favor. A judge crawled out of bed and arraigned him in the dead of night. Morton never saw the inside of a jail cell. He's probably out celebrating right now."

West's heart stopped in his chest. He couldn't have heard correctly. "What? Are you kidding me? He's out? How long has he been free?"

Faulkner sighed tiredly. "Four or five hours maybe. Shit, I just found out about it ten minutes ago. I'm not any happier about it than you are. My balls are in a wringer over here about the bust as it is. The powers that be are threatening to demote me down to dog catcher."

This wasn't Faulkner's fault but that didn't make things any better. Gigi was out there…somewhere. Unprotected and on her own.

"Gigi left alone for the coffee shop. I have to go find her."

West didn't wait another second, ending the call and shoving his feet into a pair of tennis shoes before bolting out of the room and into the nearest elevator. The ride seemed to take twice as long as it had last night and the doors had barely opened when he dashed into the lobby, his breathing ragged with full-on terror. He couldn't let anything happen to Gigi, not after all she'd been through to hide from that psycho-bastard.

Shoving open the hotel doors, he ran onto the sidewalk and straight into the coffee shop only two doors down. The customers must have thought he was some kind of lunatic when he made his entrance. He hit the door so hard it flew back on its hinges and slammed into the wall while he stood there, panting and a wild look on his face. His gaze darted from corner to corner but Gigi was nowhere to be found.

He backed out of the door and stood on the sidewalk, barely controlling the urge to yell her name at the top of his lungs. She wasn't in the coffee shop and if she'd been walking back he would have ran into her. *She was gone.*

He stumbled a few steps back toward the hotel but stopped when he saw something out of the corner of his eye. Kneeling down, he scooped up the broken pieces of Gigi's cell phone in his palm. The pink flowered case was split and cracked but there was no doubt this was hers. He'd helped her pick it out in the early days of their relationship, teasing her about how girly it was. She'd taken his crap and simply stuck out her tongue in response and giggled.

He'd give anything to see her do it again right this minute.

The sound of running footsteps caught his attention and he looked up to find Travis and Zach standing over him, wearing puzzled expressions.

"What's going on? Where's Gigi?" Travis asked as West stood in shock holding what was left of her phone.

"I don't know where she is but I don't think she would give this up willingly." West held out his hand with the broken phone and Zach's face turned pale.

"Fuck, he's got her, doesn't he? When did he get out of jail?

When I find him he's going to wish he'd never been born."

"I think we all want a beat down on this guy," Travis replied, retrieving his cell from his pocket. "I'm calling Jason and we need to call Faulkner. Maybe the police too."

"I'm going to kill Morton." West's tone was quiet but deadly, matching his mood. He didn't know what this sick fuck was going to do and he didn't want to wait around to find out. But running off half-cocked wasn't smart either. They needed to figure out where Morton would take her and then put together a plan that wouldn't get her and the rest of them killed.

"Easy, little brother. We're going to find her. I promise."

West had promised Gigi last night that everything was going to be alright and somehow he'd fucked up. He should have kept her close until...shit, after the trial? Gigi would never have put up with that. But he couldn't shake the feeling that this was all his fault. He'd let her down and now she was in that bastard's clutches again.

"How can I help?" Zach's jaw was tight and his shoulders stiff as he crossed his arms over his chest. "I want in on this. Don't leave me out. I can handle myself."

"We're going to need every man we can get," West assured him. "No one gets left behind."

A promise was a promise. West would get Gigi back from Morton if it was the last fucking thing he'd ever do.

Chapter Twenty-Six

ALAN HAD LOCKED Gigi and Aubrey in the basement of an older home out in the suburbs. They'd driven for a long time, Alan keeping up a one-sided conversation about his efforts to find her the last two years. Gigi refused to respond but that didn't stop him from explaining how he'd tracked down Zach in Las Vegas and Aubrey in Chicago, even going so far as to hire her away from her last job so he could keep an eye on her.

He was a diabolical asshole who was also clearly a psychopath. It had never occurred to him in the last few years to simply give up and move on. He'd made it clear…he'd never let her go.

The basement had a living room and small kitchen plus a separate bathroom in the corner. Gigi had already climbed up on a table under a tiny window and tried to push it open, but it was jammed closed and refused to budge no matter how hard she shoved. She and Aubrey had combed through every cabinet and drawer looking for a screwdriver, hammer, or anything that they could use to pry the window open. Or break it. Gigi wasn't fussy about how they escaped.

"I thought I'd dodged death last night but now I'm not so sure," Aubrey sighed, falling into the couch cushions a defeated expression on her face.

"You almost died last night?" Gigi paused her search under the kitchen sink, alarmed at her sister's statement. "Is that when Alan kidnapped you?"

"No, he didn't get me until this morning when I came into the office." Aubrey shook her head and nervously pushed a stray strand of hair behind her ear. "Last night I was at Alan's club and when the police came in there were shots fired. An incredibly handsome man pushed me to the floor and kept me down there until the action died down. He may have saved my life."

"That was Travis." Gigi slapped her forehead as she remembered the story she'd heard last night. "He's West's older brother and a great guy. He had a cut on his forehead and he told us a story about pushing a woman to the floor and her jewelry cutting him."

Aubrey held up her right hand and displayed a silver filigree ring on her pinkie. "It must have been this. I honestly didn't realize he was hurt. I was kind of freaked out and may have not thanked him properly."

"It was a small cut," Gigi assured her sister, coming to sit next to her on the sofa. "You can thank him when he and West come to our rescue. I know they're trying to find us right now."

Gigi had no doubt at all that West was in a frenzy trying to find her. The only question in her mind was if he would succeed. She didn't know where she was so how could he? Alan had never brought her here in the past and she wasn't aware of any connection to this house. He could have purchased it just for this one purpose – keeping her prisoner.

Aubrey hopped to her feet and began to pace the floor as she wrung her hands together. "All these months that I've been working for Alan and this is why he wanted me. He was a pretty lousy boss too. He was weird and lately he'd been given to fits of temper. I was actually planning to look for a new job. And all this time he really only wanted to use me as bait to trap you. I feel so awesomely stupid. I should have known when he hired me away from my last job. I'm a good assistant but there's nothing special about me."

"Alan fooled me as well. When I first met him I thought he was a nice guy who really cared about me. It was only as time went on that I truly began to see what and who he really was. He's good at hiding his intentions. Don't feel badly, Bree. He's had lots of practice at this. He's an expert." Gigi rubbed her damp palms against the denim of her jeans. "I'm just so sorry you were dragged into this. So very sorry. I made the mistake of telling him that I wanted to find you and look how things ended up."

Aubrey quickly sat down beside Gigi and pulled her into a hug. "We've found each other again and for that I can't be sad. I never forgot you and Zach." Her smile widened and she took a deep breath. "I can't wait to meet him. Has he changed a lot?"

"Actually, he looks the same except older. Same hair and eyes. He's quite handsome. I bet he has a lot of girlfriends. Remember how the girls in his class would always have crushes on him? He'd always get the most valentines at school."

Aubrey giggled and sat back into the cushions, a smile on her lips. "I'd forgotten that until you mentioned it. My new family didn't want me to think about the past very much so I learned not to talk about it."

Gigi and Aubrey had quickly caught up on each other's lives when they'd been dumped into this locked room. Like Zach, Aubrey had been adopted into a new family which explained her changed last name.

"That's kind of sad but not a surprise. Even at the group home they encouraged concentrating on the future and not dwelling on the past."

Aubrey's expression softened. "I'm sorry that you didn't find a family."

Gigi had made her peace with that part of her life. "Me too, but it just wasn't in the cards. The first foster family I was with wanted to adopt me but then they got a divorce so I was shuttled off to the group home. It wasn't a bad place. They were good to me. I've heard some real horror stories and I don't have any of those."

Smiling, Aubrey squeezed Gigi's hand. "From what you told me about West you'll be a family with him, and he has parents and brothers and sisters. You'll have that big happy family we always dreamed about."

Gigi had deliberately stopped dreaming about having a home when she was in her teens. Not wishing for things that would never happen made her day to day life easier. It was only when she'd held on to hope that she was frustrated and sad.

"We'll see," Gigi replied, still not sure she had what it took to create a family and home. West had promised they'd learn together but then he at least had good examples to follow. What did she have? Families she'd seen on television. Books she'd read. "We have to get out of here first or neither one of us will be planning any happily ever afters."

Shuddering with what had to be fear, Aubrey wrapped her arms around her torso. "Is he going to kill us? Just tell me the truth. Don't baby me because I'm your younger sister."

Swallowing down the acid she'd been choking on since the moment she'd seen Alan again, Gigi shook her head. "I don't honestly know. He always said that if he couldn't have me that no one else would either. If he found me he has to know that I'm with West now. Alan won't be happy about that and he can be violent when he's angry. I've seen him do terrible things to some of the men that work for him."

"He wants you but...me? I've served my purpose," Aubrey said, her tone laced with bitterness and despair. "I was the bait and now he doesn't need me anymore. You shouldn't have given in and climbed in the car. You should have run when you had the chance. I'm dead either way."

Gigi swung around and grabbed her sister by the forearms and gave her a little shake. "Stop that shit. Just stop it. No one is going to die here. We're going to get out. And as for leaving you, think again. We may not have seen each other in years but you're my sister and I wouldn't leave you with that monster for anything in the world. Do you understand me? We've got to stay calm and work together."

Aubrey's eyes were bright with unshed tears but she bravely nodded her head. "I understand. Together. We can figure this out, right? There has to be a way out of here."

The sound of the door at the top of the stairs made both of them look up where Alan was descending the steps a cynical smile on his face. He'd changed in the last few years. When she'd met him she'd thought he was boyishly handsome but now his jaw looked weak and his face bloated. She couldn't fathom how she'd been attracted to him once upon a time.

"Ladies, I hope you're finding your accommodations comfortable?"

That mocking tone never ceased to make her want to smack that smirk right off his face. He must have read her thoughts because he raised an eyebrow as he reached out to touch her hair. She jerked away and for a moment anger flared in his eyes but then he quickly hid it, smiling mildly as he leaned against one of the armchairs.

"Aubrey, I'm going to take your sister upstairs and give her a tour of the house." He pulled a folded newspaper out of his back pocket and tossed it on a sofa cushion. "Here's something to keep you occupied while she's gone."

"I won't lea–" Gigi began but Alan slammed his fist down on the coffee table, scaring her into silence. She inwardly trembled but hoped he couldn't see the real fear inside. If he knew she was scared there wouldn't be any doubt he had the upper hand.

"Don't worry, you'll see each other again. You'll be together again before you know it. Now stand up and come with me."

Gigi reached for Aubrey's hand. "I'll be back."

"Of course you will. You worry too much, Aubrey."

That fucking tone again.

His fingers clamped painfully around her upper arm and she had to grit her teeth not to wince. She'd learned in the last few years men like Alan only understood power and weakness. He had to be one hundred percent in control and that was the one thing she'd never let him have. Not anymore.

Alan was going to find that the Gigi that had run out of here wasn't the woman he'd dragged back. Somehow she'd find a way to get Aubrey and herself out of this alive.

West? If you're out there, I need you. I love you.

✦ ✦ ✦

THE UPSTAIRS OF the home looked like it had been furnished sometime in the seventies or eighties and hadn't been updated since. The living and dining room combination was decorated in a hideous dusty rose color while the kitchen was painted a china blue with checkered curtains on the windows overlooking the large backyard. The dining table would easily accommodate eight hungry diners or even ten if they scooted close. Gigi hadn't seen the upstairs, but based on the size of the lower level and the basement this house had once belonged to a large family.

She wandered over to the fireplace and let her gaze linger on the framed photos sitting on the mantle. A black and white of a young woman with a beaming smile. Smaller photos of several blond-haired children. A large one of a family – mother, father, and six happy children all dressed up in their Sunday best. Gigi stiffened in shock when she recognized one of the boys in the picture.

Alan.

Licking her lips, she struggled to keep her expression bland while her insides churned. "Was this your family's home, Alan?"

He'd come to stand right behind her and she had to suppress the shudder of revulsion at his proximity. Showing any emotion right now was a very bad idea.

"I see you recognize me. Do you see anything else in these photos that catch your eye?"

At first she shook her head but then the picture at the far end of the mantel came into view. It was of a young woman in a sundress, laughing and smiling at what looked like a picnic. She had long blonde hair, delicate features, and a slim figure.

It was like looking in a mirror.

Whoever this girl was she looked a hell of a lot like Gigi. Her breath quickening, she went back and took a closer look at the other pictures, realizing the girl was in a few more but at a younger age. Gigi stepped closer to the last photo and studied every detail. By the style of the dress it had to have been taken about twenty years ago. Gigi reached out a hand to touch the picture but then snatched it back.

Touching wouldn't answer the burning question that was making her temples ache. Alan was silent behind her…waiting. They both knew what Gigi was going to ask. Now or later. It didn't matter when. The silence seemed to stretch on and on, the tension growing into a palpable wall. The bastard was planning to wait her out. She wasn't going to get to see Aubrey again until she gave in.

"Who–Who is she?"

The words came out choked and tightened her hands into fists to keep from screaming what she really wanted to say to him. She was holding on to her control by a thread.

"My stepsister."

Alan reached around her and lifted the frame from its place on the mantel. Gigi flinched slightly as his arm came in contact with the bare skin when she'd pushed up her sleeves. Her stomach twisted and her heart accelerated but she didn't step away as she knew he was daring her to do.

"Your sister? I don't understand, Alan. If she's your sister, where is she?"

Alan stared at the picture, completely absorbed. He walked a few steps away and sat down in a chair, his gaze never leaving the photograph. His fingertips lovingly traced the girl's face before he looked up at Gigi.

"Not my sister. My stepsister. My father married her mother and we moved into this house with her other four children. Anna and I were the oldest. I was sixteen and she was fifteen. The moment I saw her for the first time I fell in love. She was perfect and I knew we'd be together forever."

Except that Gigi had never seen this person the entire time she'd been with Alan. A sense of foreboding filled her with dread but she forced herself to ask one more time.

"She's very pretty. How come I've never met her?"

Alan placed the frame on the end table, running his fingers along the edge as if he were caressing someone very beloved.

"Because she's dead. Anna is gone. She didn't love me. She said she would never love me." His gaze swung to Gigi, its intensity rooting her to where she stood. "Why did you leave me, Georgette? Why?"

Swallowing hard, Gigi took a deep breath to slow her racing heart. She could lie, of course. She'd done it before when she was with him. Anything to keep him from losing his temper. But everything inside her rebelled at the mere idea of doing it again. She'd come so far. Too far really to go back. She could never let him think she would be under his control again.

"I had to be free, Alan. Everyone deserves to have a life."

He scowled and picked up the frame. "I wanted to keep you

safe. She said the same thing, you know. About life. Now she's gone. I won't let the world hurt you like it did her."

Slowly, so she wouldn't spook him, she stepped over to the couch and lowered herself onto one of the cushions. "I have a life. A job. People who care about me. I won't be happy locked up in a room dressing in the clothes you've chosen and reading the books you've picked out. I won't live like that."

The last sentence had come out forcefully and now Alan was giving her a narrow-eyed stare as if trying to figure out where she'd found the courage to speak to him that way. He'd never liked being contradicted.

"This is all because of that man. He's made you think this way."

"No. I felt this way long before I met West. This isn't about him. This is about me. *Me.* I'm sorry you lost your sister but trying to control my life isn't going to bring her back, Alan. I'm not Anna."

His lips twisted as he placed the frame on the table. "Are you in love with him? Do you want to marry him?"

He wasn't hearing what she was saying but that was nothing new.

"I'm not Anna," she repeated. "You can't fix things by exchanging my life for hers. I won't allow you to do that to me. Not again."

Alan stood and walked over to the picture window that overlooked the lush lawn and the stately oak trees. "You could learn to love me again. In time. You loved me once."

She'd been a lonely, scared child who had reached out to the first person who had shown her kindness and attention. It had been more desperation than love but she had been fond of him.

Until she'd seen what he was capable of.

"No," she said softly. "I have some good memories from when we first met but our time has passed. Let me go, Alan. Let Aubrey go. Move on with your life. Holding on to what was isn't healthy. Let Anna rest in peace."

Her gaze landed on the faded photograph and a shudder ran down her spine. His obsession was frightening. He'd held onto it for years, never wavering in his determination. It was sick and twisted, and the chances of him taking her advice were probably zero. He'd never give up on this – or her.

He turned back to Gigi, his expression remote. She'd seen this behavior before and nothing good ever came of it. He was retreating into himself, the fury simmering just underneath the surface until he finally lashed out, determined to hurt others as much as he hurt inside.

"You love him, don't you?"

"This isn't about—"

Alan was across the room and jerking her up from her spot on the sofa before she could finish. He shook her hard, her head snapping back with the force and sucking the oxygen from her lungs.

"Goddamit, answer me. Do you fucking love him?"

Gigi had been running from truth and love for so long she almost let a lie fall from her lips. But something deep inside of her had shifted these last several days. West had stood by her, believed in her, loved her, protected her with his own life. Saying she didn't love him would have been the worst kind of untruth. Because she loved West so deeply and completely Alan would see through her obfuscation in a minute. There wasn't any point in trying to cover up what was plainly written on her face.

Her glib answer stuck in her throat and she had to close her mouth and start again. She took a few deep breaths to calm her racing heart as his fingers bit into her flesh. She'd have bruises tomorrow.

"Yes. Yes, I do."

His hands fell away and he took a couple of steps back. Scowling, he shook his head as if he were greatly disappointed in her. Like a parent and a misbehaving child.

"I wish you didn't feel that way, Georgette. I truly do." He walked over to the credenza in the corner and pulled open a drawer, drawing out a handgun. "All I've done is love you all these years. Since the first moment I saw you I knew you were meant for me. You're mine. Come with me."

Alan was going to keep the promise he'd made long ago. If he couldn't have her no one would.

Chapter Twenty-Seven

W EST SCRUBBED HIS fingers through his hair and tried to hold onto what last vestige of control he had. He needed to find Gigi and Agent Caleb Faulkner had assured him that he would help. After giving the federal agent the bare bones explanation, West had used his newfound knowledge of Alan Morton to try and ascertain where he might take her.

That had led him to the dossier that Jared had sent this morning. West had found an entry showing that Morton had purchased his childhood home right after Gigi ran from him. It was the most logical place to take her.

That's why West was standing here on the sidewalk in front of the hotel waiting for Faulkner to pick him, Zach, and Travis up and drive them to the location.

Since all three men were unfamiliar with Chicago and its suburbs they wouldn't be saving any time trying to find it on their own. It was difficult to make himself wait even the ten minutes for Faulkner to arrive but West reminded himself that he needed to keep his feelings under control if he was going to be any help to Gigi. An emotional mess wasn't what she needed right now.

A sedan with tinted windows pulled up to the curb and the passenger side window slowly lowered.

"Let's go."

The voice of Caleb Faulkner could easily be heard over the city sounds and West didn't hesitate, sliding into the front seat with the agent while Zach and Travis took the back. The vehicle darted forward, tires squealing and throwing West back in his seat. He couldn't say Faulkner didn't have a fucking sense of urgency. The man had barely pulled away from the hotel and had already pressed the accelerator to the floor in some nasty Chicago traffic.

Unfortunately it didn't help West breathe any easier, perspiration running down his neck. Nothing would be right until he could see Gigi was unharmed.

"I've already called for backup at the suspected location plus put a BOLO out for Morton's limo. I've got agents staking out his mansion but at the moment it appears to be empty. If Morton has your girl he didn't take her there. Now tell me again why you think he took her to a house in Oak Brook."

"My research guy got some background on Morton this morning," West said. "I think I know why he's so focused on her."

The car weaved in and out of traffic, barely missing the rear bumper of a Porsche that was doing the same.

"I'm listening."

West dearly hoped Faulkner could do that and drive at the same time. Otherwise they wouldn't be alive long enough to find Gigi. The man was a menace on these vehicle clogged roads. They already had three near-death misses in the last ten minutes.

"My friend sent me pictures of Morton's family. Gigi could be his stepsister's twin. From what Jared was able to glean the guy was obsessed with her. She wasn't as enamored and then a few years later died in a car accident. I doubt he's been right in the head since. He certainly isn't acting sane."

"What does that have to do with this house in Oak Brook?"

"It's his childhood home," West replied through gritted teeth, his fingers clamped onto the dash as the sedan crossed three lanes of traffic to take an exit. "He purchased it right after Gigi ran away from him. Her absence must have kicked his obsession into a higher gear. If he's trying to recreate his life with his sister Anna, then what better place to take Gigi than where he lived? Besides, I can't just sit here with my thumb up my ass and wait. This lead is the most solid."

"I can't argue with the logic," Faulkner agreed, finally slowing down for gridlocked traffic. Now that they were almost at a standstill, West was actually missing the agent's devil-may-care driving skills. "I will say that he never mentioned his sister or anyone named Anna the entire time I was undercover. Do you both agree the house is the best play?"

Travis and Zach nodded in agreement.

"I think we're on to something," Zach replied. "And I'm like you, West. I can't just stand here and do nothing."

Travis grinned. "I'm with you, little brother. You're the cop."

Everyone was supporting West's decision, so he could only hope that he was right. Because if he wasn't and something happened to Gigi...

Alan Morton would wish he'd never been born.

✦ ✦ ✦

GIGI TUGGED AT the metal handcuffs but all she succeeded in doing was cutting into the flesh of her wrists. At gunpoint Alan had forced her into this car in the garage, cuffing her to the door handle in the backseat. All the while he'd been muttering something about saving Gigi from herself but she hadn't heard much of what he'd said. She'd been too busy yelling and screaming the place down. If he wanted to shoot her then he should get on with it and stop fucking around.

"Shut up," he growled as she threw her head back and gave another banshee yell. "Nobody's going to be able to hear you anyway once I start the engine."

That got her immediate attention.

Was he planning to gas her to death? A cold sweat broke out over her skin, making her shiver with fear. She didn't want to die. She'd fought for too long to give up now.

"You're going to kill me? Let me die here? That's low, Alan, even for you."

Alan leaned against the garage wall, a curiously blank expression on his face that sent chills down her spine. It was as if his humanity had drained away and the id of his personality was fully in charge.

"You've left me no choice, Georgette. You won't let me take care of you. Save you. You love him just like Anna. It's what killed her, her love for him. I told her not to go out with him but she didn't listen. Just like you."

The words came out in a flat monotone. No inflection. No emotion. Was Alan's pain so deep that he had to shut off every feeling to be able to handle it?

"Killing me won't bring her back," Gigi said, desperate to stall or try to reason with him. Anything to keep him from carrying out his evil plan. "You're not a killer, Alan. You're better than that. Don't do this."

Gigi deliberately didn't mention her sister Aubrey still locked in the basement. In the almost catatonic state he was in he might have forgotten about her. She would live even if Gigi died.

"I have no choice," he repeated, his eyes gone cold and lifeless. "You don't know how much I miss her every single day."

Keep him talking. Delay. Focus.

"You must have loved her very much."

Every ounce of discipline she'd harnessed these last two years on the run was scraped together in that instant. She sounded almost calm as if she faced death every day and it was no big deal. She kept her tone low and soothing just like she'd heard West talk to a skittish horse at his ranch. Despite a heartbeat that sounded like a freight train in her own ears, she held on to the last shred of control she had left.

"She never loved me." Alan shook his head. "Not like I loved her. When my dad married her mom it changed my life."

"You—you had a family after that." The words stuck in her throat already tight with terror. "I never really had one. You're lucky. Not everyone gets to experience it."

"Family will hurt you if you let them. I won't let that happen to you."

"But you're hurting me if you do this," Gigi said urgently, tugging at the cuffs again. "I'm begging you to stop this. Anna's gone and nothing will bring her back."

"I don't want to talk about this anymore." Alan straightened and stomped out of the garage but Gigi sighed in relief. He hadn't started the vehicle so perhaps he had changed his mind. While he was gone she tried to tear off the door handle or unlock the cuffs but she was locked in tightly. Only a key was going to budge them.

The door leading to the house swung open and Aubrey stood in the opening, her face pale and her lips trembling. Gigi didn't have to see behind her to know that Alan was standing there holding a gun to Aubrey's back. It was clear by the stiff way she held her body and the slight shake of her shoulders as if she might break down at any time.

"Get in the car." Alan pushed Aubrey, who had paused next to the back seat passenger-side door when she'd seen Gigi cuffed to the handle. Aubrey stumbled slightly but managed to stay upright by reaching out and placing a hand on the car. It was then that Gigi noticed the handcuffs that dangled from Aubrey's left wrist.

"Let her go, Alan. She doesn't have anything to do with this. You might be able to tell yourself you're helping me, but if you kill her too you're just a cold-blooded murderer. Is that who you want to be?"

Fear had given way to outright anger when she'd seen Aubrey standing in that doorway, scared to death. She jerked her hands again, the sharp metal cutting into the skin and sending a wave of pain up her arms. In a perverse way the hurt felt good. Right now when she was so close to feeling nothing ever again it made her more alive. Everything around her had somehow become magnified. She could smell the dusty aroma of the garage mixed with the faint scent of gasoline. Shafts of sunlight filtered through the dirty garage windows, illuminating its dingy contents. Even the inside of the car smelled musty and old.

It was a depressing place to die.

The fake leather of the door handle was slick with her own sweat and her fingers slipped when she tightened her grip, the knuckles of her hand turning white.

"You'll be at peace very soon, Georgette."

Alan's tone and movements were robotic now, his arms and legs jerky as he snapped the cuff around Aubrey's wrist, attaching her to the door handle. He walked around the car slowly, in no particular hurry, to the driver's side where Gigi sat and she kicked out at him with her feet as hard as she could despite the awkward angle.

Not even flinching at the blows, Alan reached into his pocket and pulled out a set of keys before catching her legs with one arm and scooping them inside of the vehicle, quickly shutting the door before she could react. Without saying a word he sat down in the driver's seat and fired up the engine before getting up and closing the door behind him.

With the garage door and windows closed it wouldn't take long for the carbon monoxide to put them to sleep and then a short time later kill them. Alan stood there for a moment...-just...staring...as she tried frantically to free herself. Metal dug into her wrists but she didn't dare stop pulling at the handle, hoping it would give way and separate from the door. She screamed again at the top of her lungs, calling for help while Aubrey joined in. Finally he turned away and went back into the house, leaving them to become victims of the poison exhaust.

I love you, West. Dammit, I really love you. Now I'm going to die and not get to have a future with you.

Tears began to slide down her cheeks even as the stifling air inside the car made her sticky, her shirt clinging to her back. Happiness had been so close she could taste it but now she was about to become another statistic they talked about on the evening news.

A woman killed by her ex. Film at eleven.

How many times had she seen or read those words but their real meaning had never truly sunk in? Someone was dead at the hands of someone she should have been able to trust.

"Don't pull at the cuffs, Bree. Pull at the door handle. If one of us can get free we can climb into the front seat and turn off the ignition." Gigi gazed at her baby sister with all the sorrow she could muster. It was her fault that Aubrey was here and now in danger. "I'm so sorry. So very sorry."

Aubrey gave the handle another pull, a groan escaping from her quivering lips. "If I get out of this alive I swear I'll stop being so scared of going after what I want. But it's not your fault. I worked for him. I won't give up. I want time to get to know you and Zach again. I don't want to die."

Gigi wouldn't give up until her final breath.

She only wished she could see West just one more time.

Chapter Twenty-Eight

A DRENALINE RUSHING THROUGH his veins, West grabbed the dash as Agent Caleb Faulkner slammed on the brakes and turned sharply into the driveway of the white two-story house. The tires squealed but the vehicle came safely to a stop, the front bumper just inches from the garage door.

The seemingly innocent home was at the end of a long lane set back from the rest of the neighborhood. Quiet and secluded with a large expanse of green lawn surrounding the property, it was the perfect place to raise a family. Or keep a woman hostage.

West had a gut feeling about this house. Morton was just crazy enough to try and recreate his fucked up childhood.

Faulkner slammed the car into park and West hopped out of the car with the agent, Zach, and Travis on his heels. He ran toward the front door but stopped abruptly when the acrid scent of exhaust fumes hit his nostrils. The garage door was down but one whiff of the air told the story.

The bastard was gassing Gigi.

Zach pulled up on the garage door but shook his head when it didn't move an inch.

Locked.

Not wanting to waste another second, West's heart raced as he laid his shoulder against the front door, grunting at the impact of bone on solid wood. Built when they made things to last, the heavy slab shuddered but didn't give way. Too scared to be patient, he was about to reach for his gun and shoot the lock when he saw Travis heave a gigantic potted plant through the large picture window. The high-pitched shattering of glass assaulted the eardrums and all four men covered their heads and eyes as shards of glass flew through the air. The action left a hole large enough to crawl through if they were careful.

"Christ, Travis. Warn a guy next time," West muttered, climbing through the window, his boots making a crunching sound as he stepped on the sharp points of glass jutting from the window frame.

"Just trying to solve the problem."

He leaped from the windowsill to the carpeted floor below and sprinted toward a doorway that looked like it might lead to the garage on the other side of the wall. This time the door wasn't locked and West was able to pull it open and stumble down a few steps, the exhaust fumes slamming into him and causing him to choke and cough.

His lungs hurt as he covered his mouth and nose with a handkerchief. Making his way to the car parked in the middle of the garage West could see Gigi and another young woman slumped over in the back seat.

Don't let me be too late. Don't let her be dead.

West and Zach pulled open the door on Gigi's side of the vehicle while Faulkner and Travis went around to the other side to help the other young female. Attached to the door handle by handcuffs, Gigi practically fell into West's lap, her skin pale and her body limp. He pressed his fingers to her neck and to his immense relief felt a pulse. Steady and strong, despite that bastard chaining them to the car and leaving them to die.

West would take great pleasure in killing Alan Morton slowly. Cruelly. He would make the son of a bitch beg. Gigi and the other female had surely begged for their lives so it was only fair.

"She's alive," West called to the other men, his voice hoarse from the riot of emotions colliding in his gut. So fucking relieved Gigi was alive but furiously angry at Morton. The asshole would answer for what he'd done.

"This one is alive too." Travis was checking the young woman's pulse while Faulkner dug in his back pocket and pulled out a set of handcuff keys, shoving the small piece of metal into the lock.

"I can't wait for a fucking key. Stand back," Zach warned, pushing West away from the door before giving it a violent kick. The handle broke free from the door frame instantly and West scooped Gigi up in his arms and carried her outside and laid her on the concrete driveway. At some point Zach, Travis, or Faulkner must have opened the garage door because fresh air and sunshine were streaming into the dimly lit and dusty building.

The other young woman was lying a few feet away with Travis hovering over her body while sirens grew increasingly louder. Faulkner had called for backup while they were enroute.

The agent knelt beside Gigi and used his key to unlock the handcuffs around her wrists. Coughing and sucking air into his aching lungs, West winced as he took in the cut and bruised skin already beginning to swell and turn purple. Gigi had put up a hell of a fight.

"Excuse me, sir. Please step aside."

The EMTs pushed through and West was shoved back to make space for the stretchers. Both women were immediately given oxygen as a newly arrived police officer peppered Faulkner with questions.

Travis grabbed West's arm and pulled him aside. "That woman. She's the one at the nightclub last night. Do you know who she is?"

West shook his head. "I don't know for sure but if I were to guess I'd say she's Gigi's sister Aubrey. I bet that asshole used her as bait to lure Gigi to him."

"Do we know where he is?"

The EMTs rolled the stretchers toward the ambulance. "No, but right now all I care about is Gigi. Faulkner's got men looking for Morton. He's their problem right now."

"I'm going with you. Whether she's Aubrey or not she needs someone to look after her."

When Travis was in this mood it was pointless to argue with him and besides, West didn't disagree. They would need to talk to the female at a later time no matter who she was. West slapped Faulkner on the back to get the man's attention and then pointed to the ambulance. "Thanks for your help in finding her. I'm going. Call me if you find Morton."

Faulkner nodded and gave West an encouraging smile. "Will do. Good luck. I hope they're okay."

"I'm going with you." Zach stepped forward, his arms crossed over his chest and a determined look on his face.

One of the EMTs frowned and shook his head after rolling

Gigi's stretcher into the back of the ambulance. "We can really only take one extra person with us. We can't have all of you in the back."

"You go," Travis offered. "We'll get a cab or something and be right behind you."

Anxious to get Gigi to the hospital West didn't hesitate. He leaped into the back of the ambulance right before the doors swung shut.

"The hospital is only about ten minutes away," the EMT said, checking Gigi and the other female's vitals. "I think your friends are going to be fine."

West couldn't ask for anything more than another chance to show Gigi just how very much he loved her. Forever. If she needed time it was okay; he'd give it to her. But he wasn't going to give up. She'd become too damn important, worming her way into his heart. She was everything, and they were going to have a wonderful life together.

✦   ✦   ✦

GIGI'S LUNGS ACHED, her stomach twisted in knots, and her muscles were weak but she was alive. She'd woken up in a hospital room with Aubrey in the next bed and West sitting next to her in a chair, his forehead resting on their entwined hands. She'd tried to speak but had only managed a few weak coughs. He'd heard her though and had jumped to his feet, calling the nurses and helping her take a few sips of water.

Aubrey had opened her eyes a few minutes later while Travis hovered worriedly. Gigi couldn't suppress a smile as West's confirmed bachelor brother fussed over her sister, making sure she was warm enough and even managing to procure two popsicles – one cherry and one grape – to help their raw throats.

West had recounted the story of Alan's sister Anna and that the house had been their childhood home, but he hadn't actually said what had happened to Alan. She squeezed West's fingers and brought them to her lips, her mouth brushing the knuckles.

"Where is Alan now?" she asked, her gut twisting with trepidation. If he was still out there this wasn't over. He'd never give up and leave her alone. "He got away, didn't he?"

"I can answer that." A tall, handsome, dark-haired man swung into the room but Gigi didn't recognize him at all. "How are you doing, Aubrey? Feeling better?"

Gigi's sister frowned at the man and then tried to sit up, only to be pressed back onto the pillow by Travis. "Wait. I know you. I've seen you at the office several times. You've done business with Alan. He's always been a little afraid of you, I think. You're Caleb Deardon."

The man smiled and shook his head. "My real name is Caleb Faulkner. I'm a special agent for the FBI and my job was to infiltrate an organized crime syndicate that included Alan Morton. He was into much more than commodities and nightclubs. He had his finger in most of the gambling and prostitution in this city."

"You said you know where he is?" West stood but didn't let go of Gigi's hand. "Have you apprehended him?"

The agent's gaze flickered between Gigi and Aubrey. "After leaving you both to die the bastard waltzed into his office this morning as if nothing had happened. Of course I had a few agents stationed there just in case but I never actually thought he'd have the audacity to show up. When we arrested him — again — he acted like he'd never heard of you, Gigi, and that Aubrey was simply out of the office today because she was sick. He won't be getting bail this time either, by the way. Another judge that he doesn't own has been put on the case. He's facing not only two counts of attempted murder but hundreds of federal RICO counts."

"I hope he rots in jail," Travis growled, his brows pulled together in a scowl. "He deserves far worse."

"I saw him briefly before I came here. I'm guessing his lawyer is going to try some kind of temporary insanity plea. Morton appears to have completely lost it. He was acting like he didn't know anything about that house and that he'd never had a sister named Anna."

Gigi remembered how Alan had acted in the last moments she'd seen him. "When he cuffed us to the car it was as if he didn't have any emotions left. He was on automatic pilot, like a robot."

"A complete break from reality." Travis settled into the chair next to Aubrey's bed. "Once he realized that he'd left Gigi – or Anna as he may have thought of her then – to die it may have simply been more than he could handle."

It was over and now she could go...home. Tremont and West were home now. She didn't have to look over her shoulder anymore. A future was hers for the taking if she wanted one.

"When can we get out of here?" Gigi asked softly, her gaze meeting West's. Everyone else in the room seemed to slip into the background as she took in his handsome face that right now looked more worried than relieved. She'd put him through hell today but he'd never wavered on his promise.

"Tomorrow." West brushed his lips across hers, so light the kiss was like butterfly wings. "Right now you need to rest and get better."

She reached up and wrapped her arm around his neck, pulling him close. These words were only for him.

"Thank you for saving me. I love you."

West's face split into a grin and he pressed a kiss onto her forehead and then her cheek. "Keep talking like that and I'll never let you go. I'll have to love you for the rest of my life."

That was exactly the future she'd dreamed about.

Epilogue

"DOES TREMONT'S SEXIEST mayor want to take me out for lunch?"

West looked up from the spreadsheets he'd been scowling over to find Gigi standing in the doorway to his office. Looking amazing as always, today she was dressed in blue jeans and a bright red sweater, topped with a brown leather jacket she'd allowed him to buy her. She looked gorgeous today dressed in her favorite color. He'd learned a few things about his woman these past weeks but she'd been right all along. He did know the important things. The things that truly mattered.

He slapped the lid closed on the laptop and beckoned to the woman he adored, crooking a finger and giving her a big smile. Things had been good since they'd returned to Montana. Both of them were finding their way on how to be a couple and plan for the future.

"He absolutely does but first he wants a kiss."

Giggling, she slid her arms around his neck and pressed her body flush against his own. Those lethal curves were hell on his equilibrium but being normal was way overrated. Capturing her lips with his own, he kissed her until they were both breathless.

"Are you going to be this demanding after we're married?" Gigi asked coyly as she ran a fingernail across his jaw. His pulse leaped and he found himself eyeing the old oak desk just a foot away. It looked sturdy enough to handle their combined weight but the town founder, Jed Tremont, might just roll over in his grave. There had been plenty of funny business going on in the mayor's office these last few years with Cavendish but none of it had been the naked, naughty kind.

"This and more," West promised, dropping a kiss on her nose before reluctantly stepping back. He had a meeting at one o'clock regarding the new community center. It was his pet project and one of the campaign promises he'd made and after only three months in office it was getting off the ground. "I think you're going to need to take your vitamins, babe."

"You better keep that promise because I plan to demand a few things myself."

Gigi had never been this relaxed and happy. After Morton had been taken into custody he'd been denied bail due to being a flight risk. While in the county lock up awaiting trial, he'd had an altercation with another inmate and had been stabbed to death. Gigi had of course been shocked, but after talking to Caleb Faulkner they'd learned that Morton had been deep into organized crime. Far deeper than anyone had imagined. His death was probably a mob hit to keep him quiet.

Now Gigi didn't have to look over her shoulder ever again.

That's why West had asked her to marry him last week. He'd planned roses and champagne but the evening had ended up much different when a storm hit. They'd eaten by candlelight but only because the power had gone out. She'd still said yes and now he was the happiest man in Montana.

"We're meeting Travis and Aubrey at the pizza place," Gigi said, taking his hand and leading him out of the office. "Zach can't make it though. He's busy training with Jason. I think he's going to do well there."

Aubrey had taken a job as Travis's assistant but West was certain his older brother had far deeper feelings for the pretty young woman than simply as her boss. Aubrey appeared unaware of Travis's regard but West doubted that would last much longer. When Travis Anderson wanted something he'd do anything to make it happen.

"Your brother had the perfect qualifications with his military and security background and Jason needed more field agents, so Zach is really doing him a favor. Logan will train him up and they'll be happy to put him to work."

Gigi linked her arm with West's as they made their way down the sidewalk. "You made all of this happen. I have you and my family. I never thought my life would be like this, all because of you."

West felt the heat in his cheeks and ducked his head so she wouldn't see. Gigi kept saying this was all because of him but that wasn't really true.

"You did this, babe. You never gave up, fighting the good fight. All I did was call in a few favors. But I'll happily let you thank me again...later tonight."

West's voice dropped into a whisper at the end and he waggled his brows to emphasize his meaning. He'd never get enough of this woman. She was the sun, moon, and stars. Full stop. He was head over heels in love.

Gigi stopped right there in the middle of the sidewalk and stood on her tiptoes, pulling him down for a kiss. Right in front of the good citizens of Tremont who had voted him into office.

There simply wasn't a more perfect woman. When an Anderson man fell, it was forever.

Thank you for reading
Danger Incorporated – Hiding From Danger
Sign up to be notified of Olivia's new releases:
Newsletter Sign Up
http://eepurl.com/Y6aof

About The Author

Olivia Jaymes is a wife, mother, lover of sexy romance, and caffeine addict. She lives with her husband and son in central Florida and spends her days with handsome alpha males and spunky heroines.

She is currently working on a series of full-length novels called The Cowboy Justice Association. It's a contemporary romance series about lawmen in southern Montana who work to keep the peace but can't seem to find it in their own lives in addition to the erotic romance novella series – Military Moguls.

Visit Olivia Jaymes at
www.OliviaJaymes.com

Danger Incorporated

Damsel In Danger

Cowboy Justice Association

Cowboy Command

Justice Healed

Cowboy Truth

Cowboy Famous

Cowboy Cool

Imperfect Justice

The Deputies

Military Moguls

Champagne and Bullets

Diamonds and Revolvers

Caviar and Covert Ops

Emeralds, Rubies, and Camouflage

www.ingramcontent.com/pod-product-compliance
Lightning Source LLC
Chambersburg PA
CBHW020555180626
46810CB00007B/2520

* 9 7 8 0 9 8 6 1 0 2 9 9 8 *